MISSIONSURVIVAL

STRIKE OF THE SHARK

www.randomhousechildrens.co.uk

 # CHARACTER PROFILES

Beck Granger

At just thirteen years old, Beck Granger knows more about the art of survival than most military experts learn in a lifetime. When he was young he travelled with his parents to some of the most remote places in the world, from Antarctica to the African Bush, and he picked up many vital survival skills from the remote tribes he met along the way.

Uncle Al

Professor Sir Alan Granger is one of the world's most respected anthropologists. His stint as a judge on a reality television show made him a household name, but to Beck he will always be plain old Uncle Al – more comfortable in his lab with a microscope than hob-nobbing with the rich and famous. He believes that patience is a virtue and has a 'never-say-die' attitude to life. For the past few years he has been acting as guardian to Beck, who has come to think of him as a second father.

David & Melanie Granger

Beck's mum and dad were Special Operations Directors for the environmental direct action group, Green Force. Together with Beck, they spent time with remote tribes in some of the world's most extreme places. Several years ago their light plane mysteriously crashed in the jungle. Their bodies were never found and the cause of the accident remains unknown . . .

James Blake

James is tall and broad-shouldered, and a year older than Beck. He is fascinated by science, and very knowledgeable about the legends of the Bermuda triangle – though he doesn't believe in the paranormal explanations for the disappearances that happen there. He is not thrilled to have been dragged along on a Caribbean cruise by his mother, Abby. She wants him to go into the family business, but he is starting to become drawn to the excitement and adventure of the outdoor life.

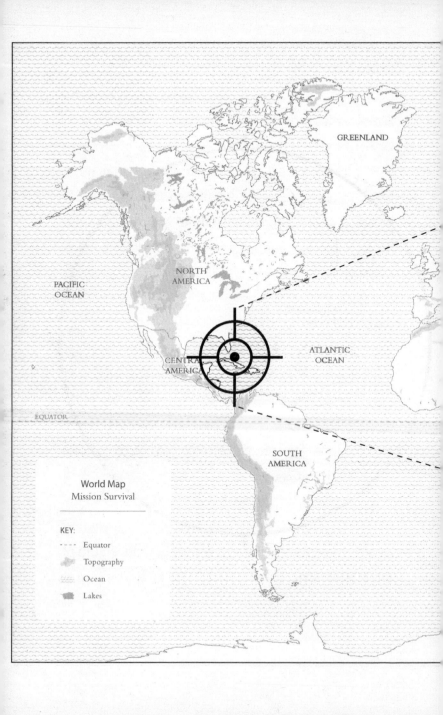

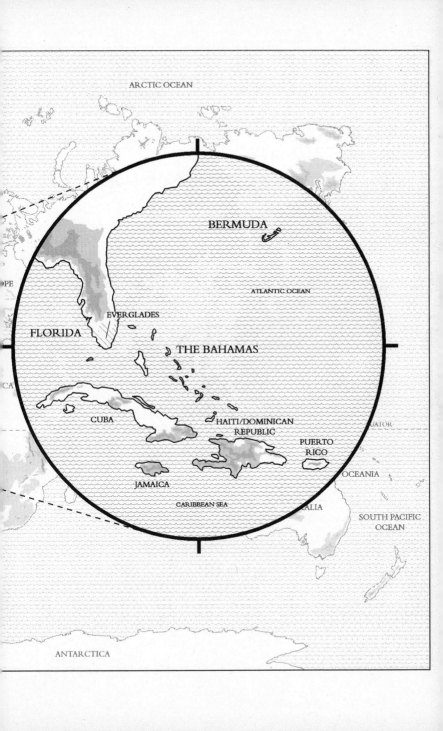

MISSION SURVIVAL

HAVE YOU READ THEM ALL?

GOLD OF THE GODS

Location: The Colombian Jungle

Dangers: Snakes; sharks; howler monkeys

Beck travels to Colombia in search of the legendary City of Gold. Could a mysterious amulet provide the key to uncovering a secret that was thought to be lost for ever?

WAY OF THE WOLF

Location: The Alaskan Mountains

Dangers: Snow storms; wolves; white-water rapids

After his plane crashes in the Alaskan wilderness, Beck has to stave off hunger and the cold as he treks through the frozen mountains in search of help.

SANDS OF THE SCORPION

Location: The Sahara Desert

Dangers: Diamond smugglers; heatstroke; scorpions

Beck is forced into the Sahara Desert to escape a gang of diamond smugglers. Can he survive the heat and evade the smugglers as he makes his way back to safety?

TRACKS OF THE TIGER

Location: The Indonesian Wilderness

Dangers: Volcanoes; tigers; orang-utans

When a volcanic eruption strands him in the jungles of Indonesia, Beck must test his survival skills against red-hot lava, a gang of illegal loggers, and the tigers that are on his trail . . .

CLAWS OF THE CROCODILE

Location: The Australian Outback

Dangers: Flash floods; salt-water crocodiles; deadly radiation

Beck heads to the Outback in search of the truth about the plane crash that killed his parents. But somebody wants the secret to remain hidden – and they will kill to protect it.

STRIKE OF THE SHARK

Location: The Caribbean Sea

Dangers: Tiger sharks; dehydration; hurricanes

When Beck is ship-wrecked in the open seas, he needs all of his survival skills to save a small group of passengers. But he soon discovers that the sinking was no accident . . .

STRIKE OF THE SHARK
A DOUBLEDAY BOOK 978 0 857 53223 7

Published in Great Britain by Doubleday,
an imprint of Random House Children's Publishers UK
A Random House Group Company

This edition published 2013

1 3 5 7 9 10 8 6 4 2

The Random House Group Limited supports the Forest Stewardship Council (FSC®),
the leading international forest certification organisation. Our books carrying the FSC
label are printed on FSC®-certified paper. FSC is the only forest certification scheme
endorsed by the leading environmental organisations, including Greenpeace. Our
paper procurement policy can be found at www.randomhouse.co.uk/environment.

MIX
Paper from
responsible sources
FSC® C016897

Set in Swiss 721 BT

RANDOM HOUSE CHILDREN'S PUBLISHERS UK
61–63 Uxbridge Road, London W5 5SA

www.**randomhousechildrens**.co.uk
www.**randomhouse**.co.uk

Addresses for companies within The Random House Group Limited can be found at:
www.randomhouse.co.uk/offices.htm

THE RANDOM HOUSE GROUP Limited Reg. No. 954009

A CIP catalogue record for this book is available from the British Library.

Printed and bound in the UK by Clays Ltd, St Ives plc

MISSION SURVIVAL

STRIKE OF THE SHARK

BEAR GRYLLS

DOUBLEDAY

To my late father, Mickey.
For teaching me the value of love,
fun & adventure.

CHAPTER 1

Beck Granger stared wide-eyed into the lights and knew what fear was. His tongue lay like a lump of dead leather in a mouth that was as dry as the Sahara desert. All the moisture had gone into the sweat that soaked his hair and armpits. Sheer terror pinned him to his chair.

The lights seemed hotter than the sun. Beyond them, he knew, there were hundreds of eyes boring into him, expecting results.

'Beck?' A voice broke into his thoughts. 'Beck?'

Slowly he dragged his attention away from the lights and back to the woman sitting on the couch opposite.

Mandy Burrows was about the same age his mother would have been. Her smile was friendly, and her voice was gentle and encouraging. She was used to putting visitors at their ease and getting them to answer simple questions. Usually her guests were pop stars, cooks, designers . . . Teenage boys were unusual.

Beck had killed venomous snakes. He had faced wild tigers. He had looked men who wanted to kill him in the eye. But nothing had prepared him for being on live TV.

Behind Mandy, one of the TV cameras moved in and focused on Beck's face. The red light above the lens was on, which meant this was the one showing the picture. All the thousands of viewers who watched *Mornings with Mandy* were looking at him.

Now that she had his attention, Mandy repeated the question.

'Beck, what would you say your first survival situation was?'

'Oh . . .' He thought for a moment, and fumbled for his glass of water. Beck had been briefed about TV interviews by his Uncle Al. Al had done many in his time. One tip had been: *If you need a moment, take a sip.* It meant that he wasn't just sitting there, looking stupid. It also put some moisture in his mouth so that he could actually string some words together. 'I, uh, guess it was my parents . . .'

A low chuckle ran around the studio, and he realized how that had sounded.

Beck forced a smile. 'No, I mean, I didn't need to survive *them*, but they took me . . .'

And after that it was easy. He was talking about something he loved – his experiences in the wild with his environmentalist mother and father.

'My parents could have just left me to stay with friends while they travelled, but they didn't want to do that; they wanted me to grow up with them. So they took me along too. And while they were doing their important stuff, I got the chance to' – he shrugged – 'to learn.'

Green Force, the organization that had employed his parents, sent them all around the globe. They had done great work, caring for their planet and its people. He had trailed in their wake, and knowledge had just rubbed off on him.

They had been working on a strategy to trap poachers in Botswana; he had been taught by tribal elders how to track animals across the Kalahari. They had gone beyond the Arctic Circle in Finland to investigate the herbal remedies of the Sami people; he had learned how to find food and shelter, surviving in the freezing temperatures of a snowy waste.

For a long time Beck had thought experiences like this were completely normal . . .

Mandy leaned closer. Her face grew grave and her voice dropped a little. She clearly thought she was going to say something very deep and profound.

'Of course, Beck, your parents died tragically when you were still very young – but your adventures have continued. One way or another . . . Let's see – you've been involved with drug lords in South America, illegal foresters in Indonesia, and diamond smugglers in Africa . . . You've lived a pretty dangerous life for a fourteen-year-old! Do you think you're in some way driving yourself to live up to your parents' legacy?'

Beck flushed. He had thought he was getting over the death of his parents. Then, recently, in

Australia, he had learned things that had torn the old wounds wide open. Things he wasn't allowed to say in public. He didn't appreciate being reminded of them.

'It's not like I try to make it happen,' he protested. 'I mean, I go to a normal school in England now, I don't travel – well, only during the holidays . . .'

Mandy nodded.

'But I keep coming across things that are wrong, and I know the last thing my parents would want is for me to sit on my backside and do nothing about them!'

He flushed again as someone in the audience clapped. Then two people were clapping, and then four – and within seconds the whole studio was applauding.

Mandy smiled again.

'Beck Granger, thank you very much.'

CHAPTER 2

'Bravo, Beck. Well said!'

Uncle Al was waiting behind the scenes. On TV, Beck had looked like he was sitting in a comfortable living room with a view out over London. But it was just a set. Behind it were walls of plywood, and cables and computer monitors, and people bustling quietly to and fro.

Al – Professor Sir Alan Granger – had been Beck's guardian ever since his parents died. Lately he had been taking on the role of Beck's agent too, managing his reluctant nephew's new-found media career.

It had all happened very suddenly when Beck got back from Australia. While there he had fallen foul of a corrupt organization that wanted to seize and pollute large parts of the Outback. They thought nothing of destroying a natural wilderness and trashing the heritage and birthright of the Aboriginal peoples living there. In the process, Beck had uncovered a priceless archaeological find – a cave full of prehistoric rock art – that had become famous around the world.

After that Beck had expected to fade away quietly into the background. Except that some reporter had noticed his name and had made the link to Beck's earlier involvement with the same organization, Lumos. A couple of years ago, after a media campaign by Beck and his friend Tikaani, Lumos had been forced to abandon plans to drill for oil in the ancestral lands of Alaska's Anak people.

The reporter connected the dots, and the first Beck had known about it was when the story appeared on the web with the headline: THE BOY WHO KEEPS SURVIVING; THE COMPANY THAT KEEPS FAILING. From the way they wrote the story, it was like Beck went around the world carefully foiling evil plan after evil plan. That wasn't how it was at all. But people weren't interested in facts . . . Since then, the phone hadn't stopped ringing.

Lumos had a well-funded PR department and powerful lawyers. They had gone into overdrive, trying to play down any connection with Beck. That just made everyone even more interested. Would Beck like to be interviewed? Be photographed for a magazine? Write a book?

And so Al had quickly stepped in. After his experience with Green Force and his own TV projects, he was used to dealing with the media. Al was Beck's first line of defence. He made sure no one took advantage of his nephew, or tried to rip him off, or force him into anything he didn't want to do. And he made sure that the payments went into a savings account for Beck's university education, assuming he wanted one.

It was Al who had thought it might be a good idea to do this interview. 'We can show the public who you really are – just a normal boy!' he had said.

Beck wasn't sure if it had worked. He was pretty certain that 'normal' boys didn't do any of that sort of thing.

'*Are you driving yourself to live up to your parents' legacy?*' Beck mimicked Mandy's gushing, oh-so-serious tones, knocking away his uncle's hand as Al gave his hair a ruffle.

'That was a great answer. You really took control of the interview. That's the way to do it.'

'I'm not so sure, Uncle.'

They had reached the dressing room and Beck pushed the door open. He stopped in surprise as a strange man got up and grabbed his hand.

'Hi, you must be Beck! How do you fancy a break in the Caribbean?'

CHAPTER 3

Beck blinked.

'Do what which when how?'

'Give him a second to catch his breath, Steven,' Al remonstrated – though he didn't seem surprised to see this newcomer. He pushed Beck gently into the room.

The man looked about Al's age, but with thick dark hair. His whole appearance was casual but smart, with chinos and a calfskin leather jacket. He had a wide, sparkling smile which Beck would have liked, once upon a time. With his new-found experience on the TV celebrity circuit, he was seeing too many wide, sparkling smiles – and learning not to trust them.

'I'm sorry, I'm sorry!' The man stepped back

smartly, still with that big smile. He held both hands up, palms out, in a gesture of surrender. 'I didn't mean to crowd you.' The smile was lopsided, though his eyes still shone with good humour.

Al shut the door behind them. 'Beck, this is Steven Holbrook. He's an old friend.'

That was enough to reassure Beck. He'd never heard the name before, but Al wouldn't call anyone an old friend if they were remotely dodgy. And so he shook hands and said, 'Hello.'

'I'm glad you could come, Steven,' Al went on. 'I was so sorry to hear about Paula.'

'Yeah.' A shadow dimmed Steven's smile for a moment. Whoever Paula was, whatever had happened, it seemed to Beck that it hurt a lot more than the man was letting on. Then the smile was back, directed straight at Beck. 'Beck, I have to tell you, my daughter is almost insane with jealousy. I told her I was coming to meet you and she begged me to bring her with me. But she's only six, so I thought it was more important she stayed in school, right?'

The smile was infectious, and Beck felt it spreading to his own face. He fought it back. He still wanted to know what this was about.

Al and Steven were exchanging slightly awkward glances, like they were gearing up to say something difficult; Steven obviously hadn't popped in just to catch up with his uncle. But what did it have to do with the Caribbean?

'So, Beck, your uncle tells me you're feeling the pressure a bit – all this fame and everything . . . How'd you like a chance to get away from it all?'

Beck wasn't going to answer any questions until he knew more. He shot Al a questioning look.

'Steven is a holiday cruise rep. He hires the entertainment acts for cruises. Music, theatre . . .'

'Lectures . . .' Steven said, with a grin.

'. . . and lectures.' Al returned the smile. 'Years ago he used to hire me to talk to rich Americans about Green Force's work while we sailed in circles around the Caribbean.'

'And I've just started with a new outfit that operates small, private cruises in the same area. So I'm looking for something to offer our customers that's fresh and different.'

'Unlike me,' Al said, so wryly that Beck had to laugh.

'Hey, you're pretty different!'

'Why, thank you.'

'How would you like the job, Beck?' Steven asked. 'The Christmas holidays are coming up – we could do it then, so you wouldn't miss out on school, and it pays considerably better than a paper round. We sail from Miami to Bermuda. Five days there, five days back, and you'll get home in time for Christmas with your uncle here.'

Beck listened quietly.

'And I'd love you to give two or three talks in that time about yourself, your experiences, survival tips . . . and about Green Force too, if you like. Environmental issues – all the things you really care about. I'm the entertainments manager for the trip, so I'll be there to give you any help you need. What do you say?'

Beck thought. 'How exactly is that getting away from it all?'

Steven flashed his infectious grin again. 'Just say that it takes really dedicated paparazzi to follow you onto a cruise ship.'

'Hmm.' Beck cocked an eyebrow at Al. 'Are you in on this too?'

'Me? No. I'll take the opportunity to get down to some serious studying without you under my feet.'

Beck thought some more.

While he liked the idea of a nice warm break over Christmas, he wasn't sure about the rest of it. He liked being surrounded by nature. And you couldn't get less natural than a cruise ship. Refiltered water. Engines burning diesel. Every meal for the next week already waiting for him in the freezers.

To be quite honest, it all sounded a bit boring. And it sounded *safe*.

Steven must have read his mind.

'Of course, you wouldn't spend your whole time on board. We'd stop off on islands en route – and we'll be starting from Florida. Have you ever been to the Everglades, Beck? They're a sight to see.'

Beck wondered if Steven had checked with Al first and already knew the answer. The answer was no, Beck had never been to the Everglades – the two thousand square kilometres of marsh and wetland at the southern tip of Florida that were home to countless exotic species. He had heard that the wetlands were being restored to their natural state after twentieth-century efforts to drain them. Green Force had worked hard to raise awareness of the damage that draining them was doing.

He knew full well that he was being bribed, and he suspected Steven knew that he knew. But . . . the Everglades!

And so he flashed back a grin every bit as wide and confident as Steven's.

'Sounds great. I'm in!'

CHAPTER 4

Beck whooped as the saw grass whipped past his eyes, only half a metre away. Warm, humid air blew into his face at forty miles an hour. It carried the smell of a million tons of vegetation. The Everglades!

At first glance the swamp looked as solid as a lawn. As if you could just walk across it. But the 'lawn' was actually tightly packed weeds growing up out of the dark water. No boat with a normal propeller could negotiate them – it would seize up in seconds. An airboat like the one he now sat in was the only way to travel across the marshes.

In fact, Beck was fast coming to the conclusion that it was the only way to travel *anywhere*. OK, it would be kind of hard to pop down to the shops in one – but still, airboats were *cool*. It was basically a flat raft with a massive aeroplane propeller at the back, pushing the boat across the swamp with the full power of its 600-horsepower V8 engine.

Forty-eight hours earlier he had been in London, walking home from school at the end of term on a bitterly cold, grey day. Twenty-four hours earlier they had arrived in sub-tropical Florida, for a couple of days' acclimatizing before joining the ship. He hadn't been able to believe his eyes when he saw a Father Christmas in a shopping mall, wrapped up warm in the traditional red outfit and hat, surrounded by small kids in T-shirts and shorts.

Beck leaned over and raised his voice so that Steven could hear him. 'It beats London!'

Steven was clutching onto the rail of the airboat. One eye was closed, the other only half open to check on where they were going. Steven usually seemed to think that the world was one big joke – most of it on him, but that was still funny. It took him a moment to remember to put the smile back on.

'It sure does!' he agreed.

OK, Beck decided, Steven didn't like travelling at

great speed in a boat that looked so top heavy it ought to fall over any second.

The tour had begun quite slowly, the airboat gliding down a natural canal while the park ranger in charge pointed out the wildlife: alligators that lurked just below the surface, or sunned themselves on mud banks, looking like part of the scenery until they moved; soft-shelled turtles lounging on logs or under the water with just their snouts sticking out. And there were more birds than you could shake a stick at.

But then came the bit Beck had been waiting for. The pilot picked up speed and the airboat headed for the swamp.

'Technically, it's a river.' The ranger shouted over the noise of the engine as the grass whipped by. 'It's not stagnant like a real swamp. It flows very slowly from north to south, and the natural vegetation filters it. The water's clean.'

There was no dry land out here, apart from the 'hammocks' – small islands that were scattered around them, some only a few centimetres above water level. You could spot them from a distance because they usually had trees on them. They looked like small spinneys dotted across an open plain.

'You want animals,' the ranger called, 'you'll find them on the hammocks. I'm talking wild boar, raccoons, deer. We'll be stopping for a while shortly . . .'

Soon the airboat glided up to a ramshackle wooden jetty that stuck out from one of the larger hammocks. It was a chance to stretch the legs, take a bathroom break and – Beck was amused but not surprised to see – buy reasonably priced souvenir items from a stall. The stall was built in the style of a traditional native fishing camp, a chickee – a platform made of palm and cypress wood, with a sloping roof of palm leaves. Beck gave it points for authenticity. He had seen this kind of structure in other places. All around the world there were native cultures in areas like Florida – hurricane country – where there was no point in building permanent homes: the next storm would reduce them to matchwood, and you could rebuild them in half a day anyway.

Steven walked up to the end of the jetty and stopped dead. Beck laughed at his expression of distaste when he saw the earth he was now expected to walk on.

Steven threw him a wry look. 'Beck, these were expensive!'

He was wearing the brand-new suede boots he had bought for the cruise.

'I mean,' he added, 'these are made from calf-skin and it's a well-known fact that calves never get dirty.'

'This is how you do it.' Beck took a leap onto the dirt and scuffed his trainers in it.

'OK, OK.' Steven stepped gingerly down. 'Anything's better than risking our necks on that contraption.' He rubbed his hands together. 'Right, where are the cocktails?'

'I think I saw a bar over there. They were serving these things in, um, coconuts. With, um, four or five different-coloured liqueurs. And at least three umbrellas.'

'Beck, you're talking my language! I'll see you in a moment.'

They both knew that a warm can of Coke was as much as Steven could expect. He headed over to the chickee and Beck took the chance to stretch his legs. He was gazing out across the saw grass when Steven called him.

'Hey, Beck, take a look!'

Beck strolled over, wondering what had caught Steven's interest. The man was crouching down by a bush. Beck peered closer and whistled. What had looked like a large clump of withered grass was moving, sliding, uncoiling. It took him a moment to understand what he was looking at, and even then his brain spent a couple more seconds processing the image so that he could see it properly. The snake's camouflage was almost perfect.

It was a python, and a big one. Its body was thicker than a strong man's arm. The scales glistened like well-polished leather. It was patterned with dark brown patches the colour of rich chocolate with rivers of caramel running between them.

'It's beautiful!' he breathed. And it was. He knew snakes well enough to recognize that this one wasn't poisonous, and it was unlikely to attack a human.

Steven obviously knew this too, which gave him credit points in Beck's eyes. He was fussy about getting his smart new shoes dirty but he knew something about the wild.

Even if the python did attack, it was slow: any human just had to walk away. Though if it *did* manage to catch him, it wouldn't end well – a big one like this could crush a grown man to death. At the moment, this particular python just looked like it wanted all the humans to be somewhere else.

'I didn't know there were pythons in Florida,' Beck said.

'There aren't.' The ranger had come over to join them. 'Or there *weren't*. Then some jackass goes and imports them as exotic pets, and some escaped, or they were just turned out when they got too big to be cute . . . and next thing you know, they're an invasive species. They're really giving the alligators a run for their money.'

Other tourists were gathering around now, with 'Oohs!' and 'Ahs!' and flashing cameras. The snake shifted and lifted its head. Its forked tongue flicked in and out as it studied the crowd.

Beck knew that snakes are sensitive to vibrations. When you're walking through a snake-infested area, the safest thing to do is tread heavily. Snakes will take the hint and move out of the way before you even see them. This snake must have decided it didn't like all the vibrations coming off a group of chattering, camera-flashing tourists, and it slowly started to uncoil.

'Hey, fella, don't worry. No one's going to hurt you.'

Before Beck could stop him, Steven reached out to tickle the snake under its chin. The snake reared its head back, its jaws gaped – and it sank its teeth into Steven's hand.

CHAPTER 5

Steven yelped. He tumbled onto his back, clutching his hand. The surrounding tourists gasped and took several steps back. A small boy burst into tears and was quickly hushed and comforted by his mother.

The snake didn't follow through with its attack. It had achieved its aim, which was to make Steven retreat. Steven stared down at his hand. Several red pinpricks were blossoming on his skin. Then, to Beck's surprise, he laughed.

'Well, that shows me!'

The father of the crying child had come to help calm his son down. 'Hey, there, it's OK. Daddy's going to make it all better. Look, Daddy's going to show the nasty snake. See? Hey, snake, get out of it!' And he kicked out at the snake.

Beck shouted in alarm, an involuntary cry of protest, but the snake flinched away just in time and the man's foot missed. He stepped forward again, but Beck ran across and stood in front of him.

'Leave it alone!'

'Leave it alone?' The man glared down at him. 'You screwy in the head, kid? That thing attacked the guy!'

The ranger was suddenly at Beck's side, trying to placate the man. 'Sir, please . . .'

Beck turned back to the snake while the men argued. It was resolutely making its way towards the water. The rest of the group were gathered around, obviously not sure if they should try and do something. The snake reached the edge of the hammock and disappeared under the surface, barely making a ripple. Cameras clicked away behind it as it went.

Beck looked at the spot where the creature had been and silently wished it well. All it had wanted was to warm itself in the sun and maybe digest its latest meal in peace. It hadn't asked to be disturbed by a group of loud, annoying, ignorant humans.

Meanwhile the argument was still going on.

The father was threatening to bring in his lawyers.

'Sir,' the ranger said, keeping his temper with a heroic effort, 'can I remind you that the animals are wild—'

'*Wild*? The animals are *wild*? This is a nature reserve! You mean you have dangerous animals in a nature reserve? What kind of outfit is this?'

The argument continued as Beck rejoined Steven.

'Wow.' Steven gazed over at the angry man. 'I suppose I didn't put two and two together. Just because a snake's not poisonous doesn't mean it's not bitey. I mean, my cat at home isn't poisonous, but she'll bite you given half a chance.'

Beck had taken a deep breath to remind Steven on how to approach animals in the wild. But the man seemed so contrite – and hey, Beck thought, he had been bitten, so it wasn't like he hadn't learned anything – that he let the breath out again.

'Can I see?' he asked. Steven held out his bitten hand and Beck studied it carefully. There were a few drops of blood and the start of some bruising. The snake had just given him a nip, barely breaking the skin. Beck was pleased it had let Steven go of its own accord. A snake's teeth, even those of a non-poisonous python, curve backwards so that its prey can't pull free.

'Have you had a tetanus shot?' he asked.

'Last year.'

'Then just put some disinfectant on this and you'll be fine. It wasn't poisonous but there could be bugs in the saliva. Snakes don't ever brush their teeth, you know! There might be a first-aid kit in the stall.'

'Well, let's see.' They strolled over to the chickee, Steven still clutching his hand to his chest. His smile was a little twisted but he didn't seem to be in pain. With a wry, self-mocking grin, he added: 'You can put this into one of your talks on the ship, if you want.'

Beck pulled a face. The thought of talking about himself to a bunch of strangers still made him nervous.

'Like, what does Beck Granger advise about avoiding python attacks?'

'Exactly. So, what *does* Beck Granger advise?'

'Don't get into danger in the first place,' Beck said shortly. 'That usually works with any kind of animals.'

Though he had to admit it hadn't always worked for him. When things went wrong, it was usually because the animals in question were humans. Animals attack if they feel threatened or hungry. Humans can just decide they're going to come and bother you regardless.

CHAPTER 6

'So, this is the one.' Steven and Beck craned their necks to look up at the ship towering above them. 'The *Sea Cloud*.' The name was painted below the rail.

They slung their bags over their shoulders and walked along the quay towards the gangway.

Their taxi had dropped them off at the front of the ship. A large white bow curved above them. A pair of anchors were suspended above their heads and looked like they were poised to come crashing down. The sides were freshly painted white to reflect the heat. Ripples of light from the water threw a pattern onto the metal that reminded Beck of the python's scales.

A pair of lifeboats hung, one in front of the other,

near the stern – the rear of the ship. Beck assumed there would be another pair on the other side. The ship's funnel was sloped, giving the impression that the *Sea Cloud* was cruising at top speed even when it was dead still. A slim mast further forward carried the ship's radio antenna and radar. The ship was sleek and clean, ready to slip away from the quay-side and take them on their adventures – though smaller than Beck had expected. He had seen pictures of cruise ships that were like floating cities, with thousands of passengers and guests. This one, he estimated, was maybe 100 metres long, maximum. He counted two rows of portholes between the water and the main deck.

'How big is it?' he asked.

'Ninety metres – seventy passengers and thirty crew, four thousand tons, top speed twenty knots.' Steven trotted out the facts like he had memorized them. He noticed Beck's surprised look. 'I said it was small and private, didn't I? Al said you wanted to get away from it all. I wasn't going to expose you to thousands of gawkers.'

'Hey,' Beck said with a grin, 'that suits me!' He

was pretty relieved that he wouldn't be facing a huge crowd every night.

Steven ran his eyes up and down the ship. There was not a soul in sight. 'Looks like we're the first, though I assume the staff are on board . . .'

The gangway led up to the main deck at a steep angle. Here there was still no one around. Steven looked about him with a wide, happy smile. It suddenly struck Beck that he felt the same way as Beck did whenever he set foot in the wilderness. This was his natural environment. This was where he was at home.

'Still no one? Well, we've definitely got the right time and place! Let's find our cabins. We're on C-deck, cabins twelve and fourteen. That's the next level down.'

They walked along the deck until they found a door, and Steven was just about to open it when a voice called, 'Ahoy!'

The man wore a uniform that gleamed crisp and white, and he strode down the deck like he owned it. In effect, he did. He had four gold stripes on each shoulder, and Beck knew this was the code that meant 'captain'. There was something about the way he moved, and the stripes, that tickled Beck's memory. And then he had it. He had been stranded in the Indonesian jungle, and had come face to face with a tiger. He hadn't respected the beast simply because it had claws and teeth and could kill him. He had respected it because it was proud and powerful in its natural environment. It *deserved* respect.

The captain of a ship was like that. He was lord and master of this whole domain, and he had earned it.

The man came up to them. He was tall and powerfully built – he must have been quite an athlete when he was younger, though now he was running to fat.

'So, you must be Mr Holbrook . . .' He was American, and had a southern drawl that could make a word like 'Holbrook' sound much longer than it was. He and Steven shook hands. 'Benjamin Farrell, Captain. Welcome. Welcome aboard.' He shot Beck a curious glance. 'I'm sorry, I wasn't aware you were bringing your son . . .'

'Beck is our prime attraction!' Steven said proudly. 'He'll be giving the main talks.'

'That so?' Farrell and Beck shook hands, though the captain was still eyeing him warily. 'I understood you'd booked some kind of survival expert . . .'

Beck gave him a neutral smile. He was getting used to seeing people's faces fall when they learned that he was the expert they were expecting. He had made himself find it amusing to stop himself being annoyed by it.

'I have. This is him.'

Farrell's eyebrows went up and he looked at Beck with more respect. 'Well, hey! I look forward to hearing what you have to say. Come in, come in.' He pushed open the door and held it for them.

'So where is everyone?' Beck asked as the door closed behind them. The interior of the ship was comfortably air conditioned, and it was a relief to step out of the heat and humidity. The inside of the ship, he had to say, was not as smart as the outside. The lobby was patterned with a carpet that must have been fashionable in the seventies. The air was nice and cool but it smelled musty. There was nothing wrong with it, but it wasn't quite as swish and shiny as Beck had expected a private cruise to be.

Someone had made a half-hearted attempt at some Christmas decorations. The loops of coloured paper hanging from the ceiling looked as out of place as Father Christmas had in the mall.

'The main crew – and the passengers – will be joining us in Bermuda.' Farrell led them down a flight of stairs.

'Bermuda?' Steven exclaimed. 'I understood we were starting in Miami!'

'We do start in Miami. The ship has to get from here to Bermuda somehow. Sorry, Mr Holbrook, I assumed you'd been told all of this, because those were the orders I received.'

Steven's usual confident smile actually wavered a little. Beck sensed his irritation.

'Let's just say Miss Blake could have been a little clearer in her communications.' Beck wondered who Miss Blake was. It was the first time Steven had mentioned her. 'Our boss, Abby Blake,' he explained, when he saw Beck's questioning look.

'She's the lady whose company chartered the cruise. She said she'd be travelling with us. This is a new venture for her – she wants to see it all goes smoothly.'

'Sure, she's on board – she arrived a couple of hours ago,' the captain told them. 'She brought her son with her. Nice kid . . . a bit quiet – a little older than you, Beck, but might still be company.'

Beck had another question: 'How can you sail a ship without a crew?'

Farrell laughed. 'Most of the crew on a cruise are there to serve cocktails and canapés and pamper the guests. You can run the engines and make the ship move with a crew of six. And me. We're all aboard.'

They were walking down a corridor lined with doors. The same seventies carpet was on the floor and in places it was scuffed and threadbare. Beck assumed this deck was for crew only – they would surely have made it look a lot smarter if paying passengers ever came down here. Farrell stopped by a door with a brass '12' on it.

'And here we are. You're next door to each other.

Settle yourselves in, and if you want me, then feel free to come up to the bridge. See how we run the ship. We cast off at sixteen hundred hours, which is,' – he checked his watch – 'two hours from now.' He turned to leave.

'Oh, before you go, Captain . . .' Steven said quickly. His voice had changed abruptly. He looked from Farrell to Beck and bit his lip. Beck sensed some kind of bad news on its way and wondered what it could be.

Steven turned and put his hands on Beck's shoulders. 'Beck, are you at all superstitious?'

There had been many times when Beck had been stranded out in the middle of the wild, and he had put himself in the hands of a higher power because he knew he couldn't get through it on his own.

Some might call that superstitious. Beck didn't, because it worked. He was still alive. But he wondered if that was what Steven meant.

'Why . . . ?'

'Well, what do you know about the Bermuda Triangle?'

Beck supposed he knew what everyone else did. Bermuda was about a thousand kilometres north-east of Florida; a thousand kilometres south of that was Puerto Rico. The Bermuda Triangle was the area between those three places. It was a zone where ships and aircraft were said to have disappeared in mysterious circumstances.

He had heard all kinds of explanations: aliens, gravitational anomalies, black holes, Atlantis. Beck didn't know what he believed about the disappearances. But he was pretty sure it wasn't any of those that had caused them.

'I've heard of it,' he said cautiously.

Steven's face grew grave and he leaned closer. He dropped his voice as if he was sharing a great secret.

'Well, I should warn you that we'll be sailing right into the middle of it.'

CHAPTER 7

For a moment none of them spoke. And then Beck said, very distinctly: 'Ha, ha.'

He could recognize a wind-up when he heard it.

Steven burst out laughing. The serious mood he had been trying to produce burst like a bubble.

The captain patted Beck on the shoulder. 'Smart guy, Beck. You're not stupid.' He gave Steven a side-ways look that suggested the Bermuda Triangle joke wasn't as funny as the Englishman thought it was.

Beck wasn't sure what to make of Steven trying to take him in with legends of the Bermuda Triangle. But there was something more serious on his mind – a question about the sea that he wanted an answer to.

'I was wondering – isn't it the hurricane season?

Is this the best time to go sailing out into the Atlantic?'

Farrell looked impressed. He clearly thought it was a good question.

'Son, I know all about the dangers of storms at sea. I lost my last ship in a typhoon and there is no way I would play fast and loose with a ship's safety. Not for one second.' His voice was suddenly solemn, and this time it wasn't a wind-up. For a moment he looked like he was talking about a close relative who had died. The loss of his ship must have been a blow. 'But I can assure you, Beck, we have the most modern, up-to-date weather tracking systems on board. The thing about hurricanes is that you can see them coming, and we can move out of the way quickly before any storm hits us. In fact it's quite normal for travel itineraries to be changed at the last minute to accommodate storms.'

He fell silent for a couple of moments, obviously still thinking about his lost ship. Beck and Steven weren't quite sure what to say. Then Farrell pulled himself out of his reverie with a visible effort, and gave them his professional captain's smile again.

'I should be on the bridge. I'll leave you to make yourselves comfortable.'

'No mini-bar,' Steven said. He pulled open the cupboard beneath the bunk. 'No trouser press.' He injected a little wobble into his voice to make it sound like this was just one step short of the worst thing ever. 'Beck, this is *squalor*.'

Beck looked around the cabin, which didn't take long. He guessed it was very different to the ones that first-class paying passengers would get. If he held out both arms, his fingertips just brushed the walls on either side. There was a single bunk, and a chair, and a fold-down table. One corner was taken up with an en suite bathroom that basically held a shower cubicle. The cabin was on the starboard – or right – side of the ship, so the porthole looked out over the docks. It wasn't exactly a stirring seascape.

Beck thought he was getting the hang of how Steven's mind worked. He could tell his friend really *didn't* think much of the accommodation, but was trying not to show it: he was hamming it up to make it sound like it was worse than it was.

'I dunno,' he mused. 'I slept in an orang-utan nest once. This is pretty swish.'

Steven laughed. 'OK, OK. Look, I need to find Abby to touch base. Can you look after yourself?' He paused as Beck was drawing breath to answer. 'No, forget I said that – stupid question!'

And then Beck was on his own.

He had a whole ship to explore, and it was mostly empty. There were at least two decks below him – places where passengers would never go but where all the ship's secrets would be. The engines, the power room, the electrics – the hidden heart of the vessel. Exploring all that would be cool.

And so he set off. There were little maps of the decks at every corridor junction to guide him. They showed all the stairways going between decks, and it was easy to find the nearest one. It was just towards the stern. He set off to find it.

Very soon his way was blocked by a door across the passage. It was marked: CREW ONLY BEYOND THIS POINT. Well, Beck reckoned, he was crew . . . sort of. And so he stepped through.

On the other side everything was just plain

shabby. No effort had been made to smarten it up. Paint peeled off metal walls and it was lit by bare light bulbs. Beck passed an open metal door with a sign above it: CREW MESS. He peered in. It looked like a sparsely furnished lounge. On the table, a number of polystyrene cartons with half-eaten burgers showed that the crew of six was around somewhere. Beck supposed they were all busy getting the ship ready for departure.

He looked further down the passage. The doors on either side were all firmly shut and he didn't want to poke his head into any private rooms. He kept going past them and soon found what he was after – the top of the stairs that led down to the next deck and the engines. It was sealed off by a heavy metal door labelled: AUTHORIZED PERSONS ONLY. Beck could convince himself that he was crew, but he couldn't quite come up with a reason for being authorized. There was nobody about, so he thought he would give it a go anyway, and tugged at the handle.

'Hey! Kid! Out of it!'

CHAPTER 8

The voice behind Beck made him jump. A crewman was striding down the passage. This one was the opposite of Captain Farrell. Farrell was clean shaven and smart in his white uniform. This guy had two days of stubble and wore a grimy set of engineer's overalls. He came up and thumped a hand against the sign on the door.

'Can't you read?' He had an accent Beck couldn't place. He must have learned English from someone with an American accent.

'I thought—' Beck began. He'd meant to make a joke of it. He was going to add, 'I am authorized – I'm crew too!' but the man interrupted.

'Yeah? Think harder, kid.'

The man pulled open the door. Beck caught a

brief glimpse of a metal ladder leading down. He made one last try at conversation and found he couldn't think of anything to say.

'So, um, everything ready?' he managed.

'We sail when we sail. And don't let me find you down here again. This deck is off limits.' The man pulled the door closed behind him.

Beck pulled a face. Charming. OK, maybe the guy was a bit stressed at having to run the ship on a skeleton crew. And he wouldn't want a gawking teenager hanging around, any more than Beck enjoyed having ignorant tourists with him in the wild.

So, he wouldn't be exploring the ship's hidden depths. He looked back the way he had come. Suddenly the ship was a lot less interesting. Out in the wild, you never knew what was round the next corner. Here, thanks to those little maps, he knew exactly what there was. He remembered his first thought when Steven described the cruise to him, back in his dressing room at the TV studios. Ships were *artificial*. They weren't natural things.

He took another look at the nearest map. It didn't

just show the ladders. Up on B-deck – which was to say, the main deck, where the lifeboats were – he was interested to see a couple of large squares labelled CINEMA and SWIMMING POOL. That would be worth exploring. He could maybe do a few lengths, see if the cinema was showing anything – for the crew, even if there weren't any guests yet. There was also DINING ROOM (always worth knowing) and LECTURE HALL.

That last bit reminded him why he was here – to talk to people about survival. OK, maybe he should start acting like a survivor. What should a good survivor do? Well, first, before he even needed to start surviving, he should explore his environment so that if disaster struck, he knew what he was doing.

On a ship, any kind of trouble means you head for the lifeboats. Beck remembered hearing that one reason so many passengers died on the *Titanic* – apart from the fact that there weren't enough lifeboats for everyone – was that the third-class passengers, deep down inside the ship, had got lost trying to make their way up to the boat deck. There was no danger of that here. On the maps, coloured arrows came up from every deck to guide people to the lifeboats at the stern. There were also coloured squares showing the locations of the lifejackets. Beck decided to test the system by deliberately going for a complicated route.

Al liked to say, 'There's no protection against stupidity.' It didn't matter how clearly labelled the maps were – in a crowd, especially when people were frightened and close to panic, there would always be some who got it wrong. They would turn left when they should turn right, or go back to their cabins for something they didn't need. And so whenever the map told Beck to go one way, he went the other.

It made no difference. Whatever he thought of the state of the ship, the safety system was up to date. Every time he went the wrong way, he still found another map at the next corner, showing him the right route to take. Eventually he decided that even the thickest tourist on the planet would understand the system.

He let the maps guide him up to B-deck, where

he emerged in a kind of lobby. He was halfway down a dingy corridor lit by panels in the ceiling – though towards the bow, one of them was flickering like it was about to die. He looked towards the stern. Some of the panels there didn't work at all. And underfoot, that same hideous, grubby carpet. Someone somewhere really did have a funny idea of what 'luxury' meant.

On either side of the lobby, port and starboard, a pair of glass doors led outside. One of the panes on the starboard doors was cracked. Beck rolled his eyes at one more example of the ship's state, and pushed it open.

Whoomph. He had forgotten just how humid and hot it was outside. The moment he left the ship's air-conditioned interior Beck felt like the whole of Florida had just slapped him in the face. He ducked back inside the lobby and crossed to the doors on the port side. He went outside again, but this time at least there was shade. The ship's superstructure cast a shadow he could walk in. That was another rule for survival that he would mention in his talks – try and stay in the shade. It keeps you cool, you don't sweat as much and you don't waste energy.

Once he was outside on the main deck, finding the lifeboats was easy. He remembered them hanging at the stern, so he wandered down. They hung in pairs above the deck from heavy steel davits, two on either side of the vessel, each about five metres long. They had sturdy fibreglass hulls, and canvas covers had been fastened over them to keep the weather out. Loops of rope hung along the sides for floating survivors to cling to. He reached up to touch the keel of the nearest lifeboat. White paint flaked off on his fingertips. He pulled a face and dusted his fingers off on his trousers.

The controls for the davits were in a sealed box that was welded to the deck rail. It had a clear plastic cover. Operating the controls would be a crew member's job, but Beck was still in survival mode and thought he should know how to do it himself. He squinted through the plastic and found that the controls were labelled with self-explanatory diagrams. It was easy to work out the sequence that would make the davits swing out over the sea, then lower the boat to deck level so that people could get in, and then the rest of the way down to the water.

Beck decided to leave it there – he wasn't actually going to launch a lifeboat just to break the boredom. Tempting though it was . . .

CHAPTER 9

Beck walked on, all the way to the very stern of the ship, and peered over the rail. Once the ship was moving, the water down there would be churned up and foaming, but now it was still and oily. He turned back and noticed a staircase that led up to the very top deck – the open sun deck, where the passengers could lounge and sunbathe. He was about to head up when a familiar voice broke into his thoughts. The voice was raised and irritated.

Beck peered round the corner of the super-structure to look down the starboard side of the ship. Steven was in heated conversation with another crew member. This one looked a little more senior than the engineer Beck had met. He was dressed like Captain Farrell but with only a single gold stripe on each shoulder.

'But if I'm head of entertainment, I need to get a proper idea of all the facilities on board!' Steven exclaimed. 'The sound system . . . the layout – it's ridiculous to keep all the areas locked!'

'And I'm telling you, sir, it's orders.' This guy's accent was pure New York. 'We open the ship up when the passengers come aboard. Not before.'

'But . . .' Steven waved his hands helplessly. Beck had walked in on a conversation that was clearly going around in circles.

'Sir, if you want to argue, take it up with Miss Blake.' The man touched his cap in an ironic salute and disappeared inside the ship, leaving a fuming Steven behind.

Steven noticed Beck lurking. 'Can you believe it?' he burst out. 'They won't even let me do my job! I need to get an idea . . .' He trailed off and the usual self-mocking smile came back. 'I know, you heard me say it, right? But honestly! What is going on? I'd ask Abby, if she'd only answer her wretched phone . . . You haven't seen her, have you?'

'Afraid not.' Beck jerked his head at the stairs. 'I was about to go up to the top deck, though.'

'Oh. I haven't looked up there.' Steven squinted. 'Probably because if I was in her place I wouldn't be on the sun deck, I'd be getting the ship organized . . . Come on, let's try. So, what do you think of the *Titanic* – I mean, the *Sea Cloud* – so far?'

'It's not what I was expecting,' Beck confessed.

Steven cocked an eyebrow at him. 'Oh?'

And so Beck gave him a potted account of his impressions as they climbed the stairs. From the way Steven just nodded, and occasionally muttered, 'Uh-huh,' Beck took it that he agreed.

And then they reached the sun deck and, sure enough, there was Abby Blake. At least, Beck assumed it was her. He couldn't imagine any of the crew he had met so far lounging in a deck chair, wearing a bikini and reading a glossy magazine. She also wore a pair of dark glasses and a wide hat that shaded most of her face.

In a deck chair next to her, a teenage boy sat staring intensely at the screen of a game. He was skinny and blond, and wore a T-shirt and brightly coloured Bermuda shorts. He glanced up at Beck and Steven, and flashed them a shy smile. He gave the woman a nudge. 'Hey, Mum.'

The woman lowered her magazine and a big smile appeared on her face beneath the dark glasses. 'Steven! Darling! How lovely to see you again. And you must be the famous Beck Granger. How wonderful!'

'Abby, this is absurd.' Steven launched straight into his list of complaints. 'They won't let me—'

'Darling, Steven, I know, I heard it all. Your voice does carry when you get agitated.' Abby flashed him another brilliant smile, then put down her magazine and stood up. 'It's all right, really. I told the crew to keep everything closed up while we do some last-minute decorating and cleaning. And, Beck, I did hear what you were saying about the state of the ship and I *entirely* agree. It does need sprucing up. I promise you, Steven, we've got several days before we reach Bermuda – they'll be able to do everything while we're under way. You'll just have to be patient in the meantime.'

Steven looked like he was still fuming, but he was doing it silently now.

'If you're keeping it all closed up, how are you going to get it decorated and cleaned?' Beck asked.

Abby laughed. 'Oh, so many questions! James, sweetheart, stand up and say hello to Beck.'

The boy looked up from his game again, rolled his eyes, and stood up to shake hands. He was a little taller than Beck, a bit broader across the shoulders. Beck guessed he was probably in the school year above him.

'Hi, Beck.' He had the long-suffering smile of a teenager putting up with his mother.

'Hi.' Beck pointed at the game. It seemed a good way to find something they had in common. 'What have you got there?'

James opened his mouth to answer; Abby cut right in.

'Oh, never mind that silly game. Beck, dear, you'll never guess what I was reading.'

And she handed Beck her magazine.

He took it, slightly puzzled, and then his eyes fell on the cover. He groaned deep inside.

'Oh . . .'

CHAPTER 10

'So, uh, when was that photo taken?' James asked Beck.

The two of them were at the bow, gazing down at the water that foamed as the *Sea Cloud* cut through it. Miami was half an hour behind them and they were heading out to sea, towards Bermuda.

The front cover of Abby's magazine had shown Beck, clad in warm arctic survival gear, standing on a glacier. The headline was: BOY ADVENTURER!

'In a studio in London,' Beck confessed. 'I'm standing on fake snow and the glacier's just a big photo in the background.'

It had been a photoshoot for the makers of the clothes. It had earned a nice little sum for the ever-growing savings account.

'Right.' James laughed. 'Mum's a big fan of yours.'

'Uh-huh?'

'She's read all about your adventures . . . I have to admit they sound pretty cool.'

Beck just grunted. His *adventures*? He hadn't even meant to get into half of them, and they had showed him the worst side of his fellow human beings. Some of those he had met were smugglers and criminals who cared nothing for other people, or their planet, as long as they grew rich. Most recently, in Australia, he had been betrayed by someone he trusted and he had seen an old friend murdered. Did that sound cool?

And, far too often, the Lumos corporation raised its ugly head. He never went looking for it, but it turned up all the same. Corrupting people, corrupting the environment, all for money. Not cool at all.

As Beck wondered how he could change the subject, James did it for him.

'Hey! Porpoises!'

Beck looked down at the water. Sure enough, five or six porpoises were keeping them company.

They streamed effortlessly through the ocean, exactly matching the ship's speed and direction. They barely seemed to move their tails or fins. Every now and then one would emerge from the water and re-enter with barely a splash.

'It's just amazing how they do that,' he said out loud. 'They look like they're hardly moving.'

'You know they ride the shock wave?' James said. 'The ship's moving through the water and it sends a shock wave ahead of it. It just pushes the porpoises along too.'

'That's cool.' Beck smiled and thought of his friend Peter, who had shared some of his adventures. 'I've got this friend at school you'd get on with. He knows the science behind everything.'

'There's usually an explanation for most stuff,' James said casually.

'That's what I generally tell myself. Steven tried to wind me up about the Bermuda Triangle.'

'OK, there's definitely an explanation for that!' James laughed. He was absently drumming his fingers on the deck rail, making a faint tapping noise. 'Like, there's this famous story about a squadron of

American fighter planes that got lost in the Triangle, right? Only, if you look at the details, it was lousy weather, and they were probably flying on a reciprocal course – that's when you go in exactly the opposite direction to the one you want; I mean, a compass points in two directions and you can get confused – and so they flew away from land instead of towards it, then ran out of fuel and crashed in the middle of the ocean. No mystery.'

Beck knew all about travelling on a reciprocal course. He had done it once or twice. If a compass was pointing north, that meant the needle was also pointing south. It was easy to get confused. It was scary to think it could also happen to trained pilots.

'What about the ships that went missing?' he asked. 'I mean, if a ship runs out of fuel it doesn't crash, it just floats.'

James smiled, and the tapping started again. 'Oh, that's where it gets even cooler. There's masses of stuff called methane hydrate on the sea floor. It's a really powerful fossil fuel. Heard of it?' Beck shook his head. 'Every now and then it erupts, and giant bubbles come up to the surface. But – get this – methane hydrate reduces the density of water. Ships can only float because water has a particular density. If it suddenly becomes less dense, then a ship is just a big lump of metal trying to float on nothing. So it sinks – drops straight down. I'm betting you that's what causes most of the disappearances.'

'Scary.' Beck couldn't help looking more closely at James's hands – that tapping was distracting. A silver ring on his right middle finger was making the noise when it hit the metal. It seemed an odd thing for a teenage boy to wear.

'Nice ring,' he commented.

James seemed to jump as if Beck had caught him doing something he shouldn't, and he curled his fingers up into a ball to hide it. 'Uh, yeah . . . Family heirloom. So what's that you're wearing? Heirloom of your own?' He pointed at the light chain that showed above the collar of Beck's T-shirt.

'It's not an heirloom yet.' Beck laughed. 'Maybe one day.' He pulled out the chain and showed James what was on it: a flat metal square and a small metal rod.

James's eyes lit up. 'OK, I read about that in one of the articles Mum showed me! That's your fire steel, right?'

'Right.'

It was one of Beck's oldest possessions. The flat square was steel and the rod was made of ferrosium. Striking the rod against the steel created a shower of sparks that could start a fire just about anywhere except underwater. He carried it wherever he went.

He gave a demonstration and then let James have a go himself. The sparks gushed out and blew away in the sea breeze.

Eventually James laughed and handed it back. 'See? That's science too. Everything makes sense if you ask the right questions.'

Yes, Beck thought, *James and Peter would make great friends*. He tucked the fire steel back inside his shirt and looked at his watch.

'Well, here's one question – when do you think dinner is?'

CHAPTER 11

Dinner was served at the captain's table in an otherwise deserted dining room. There was an undecorated Christmas tree tucked away in one corner, and the room had tables for all the other passengers who would eventually join the ship. For the moment it was just Beck, James, Steven, Abby and Captain Farrell. Abby had changed into a very smart, sleek black-and-white trouser suit. Beck privately thought it made her look like a zebra. He was reasonably certain that women don't like being told they look like zebras, so he kept the thought to himself. It wasn't hard because she did most of the talking.

'And your uncle is your only family? He does sound a fascinating man. I do hope I meet him one day. Have you been in touch since you reached the States?'

'Sure,' Beck said. 'He likes to know I'm OK. I called him just before we set sail.' That would have been evening in the UK; he had wanted to make contact before Al went to bed. 'He's fine.'

'Well, you can certainly tell him you're in the hands of a *very* good chef. Wasn't that excellent?' She dabbed her mouth with her napkin. Beck noticed she also had a silver ring on the middle finger of her right hand. He supposed that made sense. She and James were the same family, so why shouldn't they wear similar family heirlooms?

At the end of the table, Steven, Captain Farrell and James were chatting. It sounded like Steven had tried his Bermuda Triangle joke on James, and was now living to regret it.

'There have always been mysterious disappearances at sea, and there's always an explanation,' the boy was saying. 'Like, have you heard of the *Mary Celeste*?'

'That ship that disappeared?' Steven asked.

'The ship didn't disappear, just the crew. It was

found drifting in the middle of the Atlantic, completely abandoned. No one on board. But there was no sign of violence – the ship wasn't sinking or anything . . .'

Farrell was sitting slumped in his chair, his expression grim. Beck suddenly realized that the subject of disappearing ships was not one that would be appreciated by a man who had lost his own.

'So, did scientists solve that one?' Farrell asked, tight-lipped.

'Sure they did.' James seemed oblivious. 'They worked out that it all came down to the cargo the ship was carrying. Over a thousand barrels of alcohol. This guy figured that vapour from the barrels could have sparked and set off an explosion. But it didn't sink the ship, and because an alcohol explosion doesn't create flames, nothing would have been burned. There would have been no sign of an explosion when the *Mary Celeste* was found. But the crew must have abandoned ship, thinking it was about to sink, and then, taken by the current, died at sea.'

'Neat,' the captain said. 'Apart from the sailors who died. Kind of hard on them.'

'Odd that you can have an explosion without any flames,' Steven commented.

'Well, there's all kinds of explosions. Like, there's this stuff I was telling Beck about, methane hydrate—'

'James, sweetheart?' Abby interrupted. 'That might be enough science for today . . .' Beck wondered if she had also noticed that Farrell seemed dangerously close to an explosion of his own. 'So, Captain, how long have you been at sea?'

'Me, ma'am?' Farrell seemed grateful for the change of subject. 'Thirty years, give or take. I first went to sea when I was sixteen years of age. It's good to be back.'

'Back?' James asked innocently. 'Why were you away?'

The captain abruptly fixed him with a hard glare, like James had asked a really impertinent question.

The boy suddenly looked anxious. 'I, uh, didn't meant to pry. I'm sorry—'

'You must remember there's a recession on,

dear,' Abby cut in. 'Not a lot of work around, even for a hard-working man like our captain.'

'The recession,' Farrell grunted. 'Right.'

Beck got the feeling that it ran deeper than that. Was it connected with Farrell's lost ship? Maybe it was hard to get another job as a captain if your last ship had sunk.

Abby went on, 'Anyway, wasn't there something you wanted to ask the captain?'

'Oh, er, yeah . . .' James gave Farrell a shy smile. 'Do you think we could look around the bridge? It sounds really cool.'

CHAPTER 12

It *was* cool. Beck decided that the moment they set foot in it.

It was like the bridge of a starship. A wide wrap-around window stretched from one side to the other and looked out into dark space. The room was dim, lit only by the glow of screens on different consoles. Two more of the *Sea Cloud*'s uncommunicative crewmen were on duty. One was the helmsman, the man who steered the ship. He sat in a chair on one side of the bridge holding a wheel that looked just like a car's steering wheel. The other crewman was moving instruments over a chart and occasionally giving directions to the man at the wheel. They both looked up when the others came in, then went back to their jobs, not bothering to introduce themselves.

Abby went to stand in front of the big window and gazed out into the dark. Farrell took James over to a console to demonstrate the controls that ran the ship. Beck wandered over to the bank of screens and tried to guess what they all were. He recognized one of them immediately: it was the radar. A beam of light swept round and round the screen. The small specks and shapes it left behind were distant vessels. There were also larger blobs which Beck guessed were islands. A very large glow that took up one whole side of the screen had to be the mainland, Florida itself, now many miles behind them to the west.

Beck looked up, out of the windows. Ahead was all dark. He stared out of the side window, back where they had come from, in order to try to match what the radar showed with his own eyes. Cheerful, sparkling lights shone behind them on the horizon. In real life, that was the Bahamas. Now they were past those islands, the ship would be heading out into empty ocean.

Another screen showed a jagged line that moved slowly across the screen. It took Beck a moment to work out that it was tracing the contours of the sea bed. He saw that there were over three thousand metres beneath them.

Then there was something else that looked like radar – though it wasn't quite the same as the main screen. This one showed large, glowing, multi-coloured blobs with no particular shape. They changed and pulsed like a balloon being blown up by someone with very little breath.

Steven came to stand beside Beck. 'Weather radar,' he said. 'It picks up clouds and rainfall and it synchronizes them with the weather reports. Look at this chappy . . .' He tapped the screen in the bottom right-hand corner. The radar had picked up a very dark mass of *something*. It looked ominous and was surrounded with little red warning tags.

'What is it?'

'Some heavy weather, if I'm not mistaken. The red flags are a potential hurricane warning, but this baby is a way off both in distance and in velocity. I'd still only classify it as a bad storm that is going to pass us by.'

Beck looked wide-eyed at the screen and Steven

chuckled. He pointed at the scale that showed how far away it was. Beck was pleased to see that it was still a couple of hundred miles off. He remembered Farrell talking about the ship's weather-tracking systems. If you could see the low-pressure weather system, then you could avoid it. That was reassuring.

Abby had begun pacing slowly around the bridge and Steven looked up at her. 'I'm still not impressed with the paintwork, but I can't deny the systems are all up to scratch!'

She stood elegantly with one hand rested on a console. She was absently tapping her fingers just as James had, and she flashed Steven one of her catch-up smiles. *Tap*.

'Well . . .' she began. *Tap*. 'Of course . . .' *Tap*.

And at that moment every screen on the bridge went dead.

CHAPTER 13

'What the—?' Farrell exclaimed into the darkness.

Beck blinked. Images of the glowing displays were still printed on the back of his eyes. They had to fade away before he could see properly in the dim red light of the bridge.

The captain hurried from console to console, pressing keys with more and more urgency. Finally he gave one a good hard kick, with no result.

He barked at the helmsman, 'Power? Revs?'

'All normal, skipper.'

Farrell seemed reassured. 'OK, we've got power. We just don't have eyes. See if you can raise Miami Coastguard.'

There was a pause, then: 'Nothing, sir. Radio's completely dead.'

'Say *what*? No eyes, no ears? This is ridiculous. All our electronics can't have just gone for no reason at all.'

One of the crew politely moved Abby away from the console where she had been standing, and bent his head over the keyboard, fingers tapping urgently.

'I reckon it's the ship's mainframe, sir. Seems completely dead.'

'And it's taken every system plugged into it. Radio, radar, navigation – oh, peachy!' Farrell hurried to the windows and peered out into the gloom. 'OK. All stop.'

The helmsman pulled on a small lever on the board in front of him. Beck had ceased to notice the vibration of the ship's engines under his feet, but he was aware of it again now that it had changed. He looked out of the side windows. The wake of the ship had been foaming and white in the night; now it was dying away. Within a minute, the *Sea Cloud* was at a dead stop, floating alone in the middle of the ocean.

James gave Beck a nudge and a wink. 'It's the Bermuda Triangle effect!' he said in a loud whisper, and Beck managed a faint smile. It was kind of off-putting to be on a ship whose electronics had all just failed – but on the other hand, it didn't seem to be sinking. As he had pointed out to James earlier, when a ship ran out of power, all it did was float, right?

'Boys,' said Steven. He still had his good-humoured smile, but when they looked at him he put his finger to his lips. 'Shh.' The message was clear: don't give the captain a hard time that he doesn't need.

But Farrell had already heard James's remark, and that was when he seemed to remember he had guests.

'Yes, very funny,' he said. Beck detected a certain coldness in his tone. A captain took pride in his ship. He didn't want things going wrong at the best of times. In particular he didn't want them going wrong in front of his boss. 'Ma'am, I'm going to have to ask you all to leave. Me and the boys have a long night ahead of us. We need to trace the fault and repair it.'

'Did you really need to stop the engines? We don't want to get behind schedule,' Abby commented.

Farrell glared at her. 'With respect, ma'am, we'd need to stand a full watch to keep sailing in the dark – lookouts fore and aft and up the mast – and we don't have enough people on board. Don't worry, we'll get it fixed. If the worst comes to the worst, we can return to port in the morning and get an expert in, but I doubt it will come to that. So, will you all please leave the bridge? Now.'

Steven gave a good-natured smile, then jerked his thumb and herded Beck and James towards the exit. 'Come on, lads. You heard.'

Beck awoke suddenly, but he didn't know why. He was surprised he had managed to sleep at all.

His cabin was dark except for a very faint wash of moonlight through the porthole. He lay in his bunk and thought back through his clouded thoughts.

In the wild he often woke when something changed. Some small clue might reach his sub-conscious and tell him that there was an animal nearby, or that the weather was about to change and there was a storm on the way – something important that he needed to be awake for. He had that same feeling right now. But he wasn't in the wild; he was in the cabin of a small cruise ship floating in the Atlantic.

So what was it? He ran through what he could hear. Somewhere at the back of his skull he picked up the noise of the engines . . .

The engines! They were moving again. That must mean the crew had got the electronics fixed. Maybe that was what he had heard.

Beck lay back and closed his eyes, then opened them again. It was no good. His instincts were still insisting that something was up. Maybe it was nothing. Maybe his wilderness instinct was just getting it all wrong. Maybe it was confused by being safe and secure on a cruise ship.

But just in case something was wrong . . . he decided to investigate.

CHAPTER 14

Beck swung his legs out of bed. The T-shirt he wore would be fine for walking around the ship at night. He pulled on his jeans and found his shoes. Automatically he slipped his watch onto his wrist and picked up his fire steel. But then he realized that, hey, he wasn't going to need it on a ship. He really only needed it to give a demonstration during his talks. So he left it where it was and stepped outside.

The passage was fully lit, and the first thing he noticed was that Steven's door was slightly open. Maybe he'd noticed the change in the engines too and gone to investigate.

'Steven? Hello?'

Beck pushed the door fully open and peered in. The bed didn't look like it had been slept in. There was no sign of its occupant, and in a cabin that small there was nowhere he could be lurking.

Beck checked the hook behind the cabin door. Steven's leather jacket was missing, so he was definitely up and about somewhere. But what would he be doing at this time of night? Would he have stayed up to help the crew? Beck doubted it. The problem had been with the ship's mainframe, and so far Steven had shown no sign of being an electronics geek.

Beck gazed blankly down the corridor while he thought about it. Then he realized that he was looking at the door that he had gone through earlier in the day – the one labelled: CREW ONLY BEYOND THIS POINT. It was ajar. He walked slowly towards it and put his head through.

'Hello? Anyone here?'

Light spilled from the crew mess into the passage, and beyond it he could see that the other cabin doors were also open.

'Hello?'

The crew mess hadn't changed, except that the uneaten burgers on the table were gone. He went to

the cabin next to it and knocked softly on the door.
'Anyone?'

He pushed the door open. The cabin had the same layout as his and Steven's. The bed was empty, the bedclothes rumpled.

The next cabin was the same. And the one after that. This was getting weird.

Beck stopped and thought again.

There were five cabins that had obviously been used. And there were five crew members, plus Captain Farrell, on board. The captain probably had his own cabin somewhere else, so everyone else should sleep down here. Even if some of the crew were awake to keep the ship running, the rest should have been asleep, preparing to take their watch later.

So where was everyone? This was like the *Mary Celeste*. Except that there had been no explosion.

Part of Beck's mind told him there was a perfectly logical explanation for all this. He didn't know much about ships. If he did, maybe it would all make sense.

Maybe they were all busy working on the

problem – gathered together fixing the electronics in the hold. So he should go back to his cabin and try to sleep.

However, he also knew that there was no way he would sleep until he had worked this out. He had to know.

If there was anyone around, then surely they had to be on the bridge. The ship was under power – someone had to be steering it. He set off at a quick trot.

Two minutes later he was staring at a completely empty bridge.

The screens were dead – the mainframe was still down. Radar and navigation systems were still out. No one was about, but the wheel twitched eerily from time to time as if an invisible helmsman was at the controls. Beck peered at the instrument panel next to it. A switch marked AUTO was lit up. The *Sea Cloud* was on auto-pilot.

But where was everyone?

CHAPTER 15

There was only one more person Beck could think of
to ask, and that was the captain. Assuming he hadn't
vanished with the rest of his crew. Where would
Farrell's cabin be?

He guessed it would be nearby so that the
captain could be called in an emergency. He hurried
along the passage, looking at the doors on his left
and right, and very soon found the one marked
CAPTAIN. He knocked, first quietly, then harder.

The door suddenly opened, and Farrell was
staring down at him. He was wearing an old vest and
rumpled sweatpants and had obviously got straight
out of bed.

'Beck? What is it?'

For a moment Beck wanted to hug him – it was

so good to hear another human voice. He wasn't the only person on the ship!

'Everyone's disappeared and there's no one on the bridge,' he said. Then he braced himself. If there was a good explanation for this, something only sailors understood, then now would be the time he learned it. Farrell would chew him out for waking him up in the middle of the night and that would be that.

But the captain just scratched his head and screwed up his face in puzzlement. 'What do you mean there's no one on the bridge? Of course there's someone.'

Beck just shook his head. Farrell grabbed a T-shirt and pushed past him, striding back to the bridge. He stopped in the entrance and stared in disbelief at the scene. Then he erupted.

'What in tarnation's name do they think they're doing? Under way with no one at the helm? I knew I shouldn't have agreed to take them on.' He caught Beck's questioning look. 'They were already signed up to the ship when I took over as captain, and the owner persuaded me to keep them . . .. *Amateurs!* I bet they're all fast asleep in their cabins—'

'Uh, no,' Beck corrected him. 'Their cabins are all empty too. I looked.'

Farrell's mouth dropped open, then tightened into an angry line. He hurried to the helmsman's position and studied the dials by the wheel.

'So who would bother starting the engines if the systems are still out . . .?' His eyes widened. 'We're at full speed!' He pulled at the throttle. It wouldn't budge. He tried again, this time with both hands. Beck hurried over to help him, but even with their combined strength the small lever wouldn't move.

'OK . . .' Farrell was breathing heavily. 'You stay up here. I'm going to go down and shut off the engines manually. We can't run blind at top speed – it's suicide. Once we've stopped, we should be near enough to the main shipping lanes that we can fire off flares to signal for help. I need to fix our position, if I can . . .'

Beck peered out of the window and up at the stars. 'We're heading due east,' he said, 'if that helps.'

Farrell looked doubtful. 'We can't be. Once we got past the Bahamas we were heading northeast.'

'See for yourself,' Beck invited.

The captain looked out of the window, as Beck had just done. Beck assumed that as a sailor he too knew how to find his way by the stars.

Beck had looked for the Plough – the giant saucepan shape of stars in the sky. You found the two stars at the end and joined them with an imaginary line. Then you extended that line upwards, right to the top of the sky. The next star you came to was Polaris, also called the North Star. It got that name because it was always in the north. All the stars in the sky would revolve around it but the North Star never moved. Wherever it was, that way was north.

At the moment it was square on the *Sea Cloud*'s port – the left – side. If that way was north, then the ship had to be heading due east.

'Right,' said Farrell after a moment. '*Right*.'

Beck tried to put himself in the captain's shoes. His crew had vanished and his ship was heading at full speed on completely the wrong course into the middle of the Atlantic. Beck could see that Farrell was about to explode with anger and frustration and, yes, fear for their safety. That 'Right' conveyed everything he was feeling in one explosive syllable.

Farrell turned towards the door. 'I still need to get to the engines. You find the emergency locker, get the flares—'

Beck felt more than heard the explosion. It was a muffled *crump* that shook the ship. Half a second later the vessel lurched as if it had just hit something or run into a massive wave. Farrell was catapulted into him, and they fell to the deck together in a tangle. Beck felt as if all the air had been knocked out of his lungs. The captain slowly picked himself up, dazed and shaking his head. Beck lay there and gasped for breath once, twice, until he felt oxygen flowing back into him.

Farrell took a step towards Beck, leaning down to help him up, and almost fell again. Beck pushed himself into a sitting position. He was leaning over to one side. When he tried to straighten up, he found that he was still leaning.

The whole deck was tilted. The ship's frame shuddered, and from somewhere in its depths came a long, slow metallic groan.

Farrell grabbed his hand and yanked him to his feet. 'We're sinking.'

CHAPTER 16

The ship lurched again. Farrell clutched at the wheel to hold himself steady.

'Engines have stopped,' he said between breaths, looking at the dials. 'Water must have reached them.' His face was ashen.

Beck's mind raced with what they needed to do. Find Abby, James, Steven, get them all to safety . . .

'We were going at full speed, Beck. With a hole in the hull, water coming through would tear us apart.

'It buys us a little time,' Farrell added, 'but not much. If the engine room is flooded already, it's worse than I thought. And it means the watertight doors aren't working.'

As Beck was about to wonder out loud what had

happened, another long, rattling groan echoed through the ship, and his heart pounded as he felt the deck tilt beneath him again.

Farrell opened a flap in the main instrument panel and smashed his fist down on the red button beneath it. Beck winced as a shrill, whooping alarm sounded all over the ship.

'Just in case there's anyone on board who's in any doubt,' the captain said grimly. 'We're abandoning ship. That'll get everyone to the boats, wherever they're hiding. Open that locker over there, get the flares.'

He jerked a thumb at the locker at the rear of the bridge. Beck hurried over, staggering against the tilt of the deck, and pulled open the doors. There was a space inside that was clearly marked FLARES.

It was empty.

Meanwhile Farrell had sat down at the communications console, pulling the headphones on.

'*Mayday, mayday, mayday, this is . . . Hello?*' He turned a dial and started again. 'It's still out!' He must have assumed that since the ship was running again, the electronics were back up.

'The flares have gone,' Beck reported.

He and Farrell looked at each other and Beck knew they were coming to the same conclusion.

The failure of the mainframe *could* have been a simple fault. The disappearance of the crew *could* have been because they were just busy elsewhere. The explosion *could* have been an accident. But flares don't go missing on their own. Add it all together and it was very, very hard to believe that it was all coincidence.

This was sabotage. Someone wanted the ship to sink without any rescue coming.

'Get to the boats,' Farrell said curtly. 'You wait there while I try and find the others – if they haven't reached them already. Go to the port side. At this angle we'll never launch the starboard ones.'

Their feet pounded on the stairs that took them down to the main deck. The whooping alarm continued to pierce Beck's eardrums. The ship's lights made the deck as clear as day, but they swamped the light of the stars and the moon so that the night beyond was just a black void. Beck had the horrible sensation that the ship was slowly being consumed by darkness.

It was a countdown until it slipped away altogether.

The deck was getting harder to walk on, and they had to sidle their way towards the stern. Beck peered over the rail and swallowed when he saw how close the sea was getting. He had wondered about going back to his cabin to get his stuff. Seeing the sea so close put that idea firmly out of his head. A wave broke against the side of the ship and washed against his feet.

Every cell in Beck's body was screaming at him to get off this sinking ship. This wasn't his usual environment. His survival skills couldn't help him if four thousand tons of ship decided to sink with him still on board. But still, he didn't want to leave if he could still be useful. He could help look for the others. He could save lives. And he wanted – he *badly* wanted – to spoil the game of whoever had set this up in the first place.

A door ahead was hanging open, partly blocking the deck. As they dodged round it, out of the corner of his eye Beck glimpsed something inside, and skidded to a halt.

'Beck, come *on*!'

'No! Here!' Beck ducked inside the door and Farrell had to follow him. He was drawing breath to speak when he saw what Beck had spotted.

Steven lay on his front in the corridor. His arms were flung above his head. He was still in his jeans and leather jacket – it didn't look like he had ever gone to bed. He was out cold . . . or dead.

CHAPTER 17

There was a large contusion on Steven's forehead and his hair was matted with fresh blood. Beck felt it, warm and sticky, under his fingers. He felt for a pulse in Steven's neck, and breathed a huge sigh of relief. It was weak and slow, but it was there.

'What happened to him?'

'Maybe he fell over when the ship blew?' Beck said. He remembered his own tumble.

'We'll hold the enquiry later, son. Come on.'

Together they hoisted Steven up so that he had an arm over each of their shoulders. Then it was back out onto the listing deck. The slope was so acute that they almost skidded straight over the rail and into the water. As they stumbled towards the stern, the lifeboats came into view. Beck's heart seemed to stop for a moment when he saw the first set of davits hanging over the rails. They were empty: the lifeboat was gone.

But the second one was still there. It had already been swung out and lowered to deck level, so that people could step in. And that was exactly what James and Abby were doing.

James was in the lifeboat, holding his hand out to his mother. He saw them and his face lit up. 'Hey, Mum! Look!'

He hopped quickly out of the boat again and came towards them. His eyes went wide when he saw the state Steven was in. 'What happened?'

'We thought everyone had gone!' Abby hurried up behind him. 'That terrible noise woke us up, and the ship was leaning over . . . We just pulled on our clothes and headed for the boats.' They were dressed as they had been the last time Beck saw them. James was in shorts and T-shirt, Abby in her zebra suit. 'But the boats had all gone, except this one,' she shouted.

'Well, help us get Steven in and then we're all going. Boys, get in,' Farrell added.

James and Beck stood in the boat and let the other two pass Steven to them. There were benches at the bow, at the stern and in the middle. The ship was tilted so steeply now that the boat hung some distance away from the deck. Beck had to reach out across the gap to take hold of Steven's head and shoulders.

He and James laid Steven out on the deck boards. His breathing was hoarse and ragged. Beck wanted to examine him properly and see how bad that head wound was.

'So you didn't see anyone else?' Farrell asked.

James reached out a hand to help Abby across the gap and into the boat. 'No. Everywhere was completely deserted.'

The captain clambered up the tilting deck of the ship to the controls that Beck had seen earlier. The crane mechanism coughed into life and the boat was lowered down towards the sea. He hurried back and jumped in before it had gone too far.

The lights of the *Sea Cloud* flickered and went out, and the crane stopped.

Farrell cursed. 'The power's gone!'

The ship lurched one more time. Another of its groans squeezed its way up from the depths, and this time Beck felt and heard something more. Sounds like large eruptions, muffled booms, came from below the water. Foam and bubbles broke the surface all around them. The waves had now reached the level of the deck, and kept going.

The *Sea Cloud* was going down, and they were still attached to it.

Farrell shouted, 'Beck! Get to the front rope! You see that handle?'

Beck clambered over to the bow, where the rope from the crane above was attached to a metal ring; by the ring there was a red plastic handle. 'Got it.'

Farrell was at the back of the boat, his hand on the second handle. 'It's the emergency release. James, Miss Blake, brace yourselves. Beck, count of three. One, two, *three* . . .'

He and Beck pulled their handles at the same time and the boat came free of the ropes. It dropped a metre and hit the seething water with a splash and a thud.

'Beck! Oars!'

They both scrambled towards the middle seat. James passed an oar to Beck, and he manoeuvred it into the rowlock on his side. He gripped the oar with both hands, dug the blade into the water and heaved. On the other side, Farrell did the same. The boat was heavier than anything Beck had rowed before. For a moment dipping the oar into the water and pulling on it was like tugging at something stuck in concrete. But then the oars bit, and little by little the boat responded to the pull and began to move away from the ship.

Abby suddenly pulled herself to her feet. 'My bag! My bag's still on board! We have to get it!'

And then Beck remembered. He gasped, and clutched at his throat. It felt bare. His fire steel. It was still in his cabin! The one companion that had been all around the world with him was going to end up at the bottom of the sea.

'There's no time, Mum!' James shouted.

Abby still looked as if she was about to jump back onto the sinking vessel, though it was already much too far away. But Beck knew that James was right. What was important was to get away from the ship.

He had no choice – he had to keep rowing with the captain. Slowly the distance between boat and ship increased.

'OK,' Farrell croaked after a minute. 'That'll do.'

They rested on their oars, and looked back.

Now that the lights were gone, the night no longer seemed so dark. Beck could see the stars. It was the ship that was black now – a silhouette on the moonlit waves. Beck watched with awe as four thousand tons of steel rolled, with massive groans and gurgles, until it was completely upside down. It was the height of a five-storey building and as long as the street where he lived, but totally at the mercy of the forces of nature. He had never felt so small and insignificant.

There goes your handbag, Beck thought silently. *And my fire steel*.

For some reason that upset him even more than being shipwrecked.

The sea continued to seethe and surge around

the upside-down hull until the *Sea Cloud* was completely hidden by clouds of bubbles.

After a minute they died away, and the ship was gone.

CHAPTER 18

For a moment there was just silence in the boat –
four people too stunned by what had just happened
to say anything. There was enough moonlight to
make out people's features. Beck looked from face
to face.

He expected the captain to take the lead and say
something, but Farrell just sat there, gazing into the
night. His jaw hung slack and his eyes stared at
nothing. He had lost a ship once before. How must
it feel to have it happen *twice*? And to know that this
time it was no accident, but sabotage . . .

James sat hugging his knees and rocking back
and forth. There was very little sign of his extra year
of age. If anything, he suddenly looked a whole lot
younger than Beck.

Abby's face was harder to read. Maybe she was too much of a businesswoman to let her emotions show . . . Then Beck realized that it wasn't fear or worry on her face. It was anger. She was *furious*.

She saw him looking at her. 'Well, Beck.' He could hear the strain in her voice as she tried to be cheerful. 'What does the survival expert say we do now?'

It seemed odd that she wasn't trying to comfort her son, but that wasn't his business. His business was taking care of all these people.

'Cut, stream, close, maintain,' he muttered. She raised a querying eyebrow.

Beck had once spent a happy weekend getting soaked and frozen in a shipwreck simulator in Plymouth. *Cut, stream, close, maintain* – the four words that the instructors had drummed into their pupils over and over again.

Cut meant cut the rope that tied your lifeboat to the ship. They had done that . . . just.

'We, uh, we need to stream a sea anchor, to keep our position.' Beck rubbed his temples, trying to massage the memory into life. He had to admit he was rusty in this area. He was usually on land.

'That's, uh, maybe something like a small parachute. We drag it on a line behind the boat, and it stops us drifting . . .'

Farrell finally stirred. 'Son, with respect, I know what a sea anchor is. It's supposed to keep you in a position where people will expect to find you, so that they can come and get you. But since we were well off course, no one will be looking for us here. We need to get moving.'

'OK.' It had been a while since anyone had contradicted Beck – and been right. You couldn't just go by the book, he reminded himself. In every situation you had to adapt.

Improvise. Adapt. Overcome. That mantra was one of his survival tenets.

OK, he thought. *What next?*

Close meant to cover the boat – get the canopy up to protect the crew from the elements. That assumed you were adrift on a wild sea full of freezing spray and strong winds. There was no need for that here. Not yet, anyway.

And *maintain* meant to keep the boat and its equipment in good order.

'We need to see what we have on board,' he said. After a slightly rocky start he could feel the lessons from the course coming to life in his head. 'Everyone look to see what they can find.'

The others stirred into sluggish action. It didn't take long.

Any self-respecting lifeboat would have life-jackets and seasickness tablets at the very least. Beck thought the ship's saboteurs might have taken care of those little details too – but no. The lifejackets were stowed in the bow of the boat. James found the seasickness tablets in a small box that also contained biscuits, and a bulging silver foil bag containing two litres of water. It had a built-in spout to drink from.

Apart from that there was the canvas cover that had kept the boat weatherproof while it was hanging from its davits on the *Sea Cloud*. And there was a tin box containing two flares. Abby found these, and displayed them as proudly as if she had been personally responsible for their presence. Plus, there was a first-aid kit. It was made of plastic, like a lunch box, but marked with a red cross; it was full of rolls of bandages and packets of plasters and sterile wipes. It meant that at last Beck could do something about Steven.

He still lay on the floor of the boat between the middle bench and the bow. His breath came in croaks and shudders that did not sound healthy. Beck knelt by his head and lifted an eyelid with his thumb. The eyes of an even vaguely conscious person will try and stay closed if you lift an eyelid. He felt no resistance, which meant that Steven was deeply unconscious. Under the eyelid, his eye was rolled right back in his head.

Beck gently probed his skull. He felt the matted hair again beneath his fingertips, and a massive swelling just below the right ear. What he didn't feel was anything moving. There was no indication of a cracked skull. That was something, at least. Even so, he was starting to feel worried. Steven had clearly suffered a severe bang on the head, but shouldn't he be showing some kind of movement by now? How hard had he been hit?

'Pass me a lifejacket?' he asked, and James handed one over.

It was like a thick, fluorescent yellow plastic bag that fitted over the head and tied around the waist. It had pockets with plastic zips, and sides made of heavy plastic mesh so that water could drain out. Each one had a mouth tube so that its owner could inflate it.

Beck blew into the tube until it was like a soft cushion and tucked it under Steven's head as a pillow. Then he unravelled a metre of gauze bandage from the first-aid kit and tied it, gently but firmly, around Steven's head.

And that, he thought grimly, was probably all he could do for him, until he woke up or they could get him to a hospital, whichever was sooner. Beck didn't like the look of that swelling. Even if nothing was broken, there could be bleeding in Steven's brain.

'Now,' he ordered, 'everyone else gets to take a seasick pill. And one sip of water.'

'Seasick?' Farrell exclaimed. 'Son, I have been at sea for thirty years and I do not get seasick!'

Beck looked him in the eye. 'If your navigator tells you to steer a certain course to avoid a rock, even if you can't see it, do you obey him?'

'Well, sure—'

'Because he's the expert at navigating. If your engineer tells you that you have to shut down an engine because it's about to overheat, even though it seems fine to you, do you obey him?'

'Of course, but—'

'And he's the expert with engines. So your survival expert is telling you to take a seasickness pill.'

They stared hard at each other in the moonlight, and then the captain shrugged. 'Sure, right, whatever, I'll take a pill . . .'

Beck handed the tablets round so that everyone could have one.

'I felt fine on the ship,' Abby said. 'Why shouldn't I now?'

Beck started to explain why she still needed a pill, but her scientist son got there first.

'It's motion sickness, Mum.' James sounded withdrawn and tired. It was the first thing he had said since the ship went down. 'Our brain gets its signals confused. Our eyes tell us we're not moving and our sense of balance tells us that we are. And so the brain puts the body on red alert, tells it to shut down all the secondary, unimportant processes. Like digestion. It's not like a stomach bug, where you're sick but get better once it's out.'

Beck remembered his instructor's words, and grinned as he repeated them. 'Right. You just keep feeling sick until you think you're going to die. Then you are so sick you hope you *will* die. Plus you dehydrate. So prevent it – take the pill.'

'I do believe you've persuaded me.' Abby took her pill. She pulled a face as it went down her throat. 'Ugh. But why should we be here for long anyway? We have these!' She hoisted the box of flares onto her lap. 'There's no point in waiting around here. We can fire these off and rescue will come.'

'From where?' James was sarcastic. 'Ooh, look! A ship! Another ship! Ships *everywhere*!'

The horizon was completely dark in all directions. Any cruise ship would be ablaze with light. Even a fishing vessel would have its navigation lights on. But there was nothing nearby or even far away. Beck knew that firing those two flares off into the dark would be useless. There was no one to see them.

'Yes, dear, thank you for that very helpful obser-vation,' Abby said, just as sarcastically. It wasn't a tone she usually took with James – but then, Beck reckoned, these were not usual circumstances. Everyone was stressed, to put it mildly.

'We should save them until there's a chance they'll be seen,' he said.

Abby snorted. 'Well, *you* can stay in the boat for the rest of your life, but I'm going to—'

'You'll do as Beck says!'

It was a moment before Beck recognized the voice as belonging to Captain Farrell. Harsh and commanding; for the first time he was using his authority as captain. 'Firing them off now would be a waste,' he said. 'We keep them safe until they're needed. Period.'

CHAPTER 19

'Well, are we just going to sit here?' Abby asked. 'At least start the engine and steer for land.' No one moved. 'Well? Come on!'

'There's no engine, Mum,' James said quietly.

Beck cocked an eyebrow up at the sky. Once again it only took a moment to locate the Plough and the North Star. If they steered due west from that, they were bound to hit America.

'Will the current carry us towards land?' he asked the captain.

Farrell shook his head. 'Out here, we're in the Gulf Stream.'

Beck knew exactly what that meant. From the way James groaned, it sounded like he did too. The Gulf Stream carried warm water from Florida all the way across the Atlantic to Europe. Beck had always been grateful for it – it was the reason the United Kingdom wasn't as cold as Canada in the winter. But right now he wished it would turn and flow back towards the USA. Just for a bit.

The powerful *Sea Cloud* had come out here at full speed. A rowing boat could go for days in the opposite direction and not get very far at all.

'Can this boat sail?' Beck asked.

'No. Oars only.'

'Then we'll row for now – while it's cool and dark. In the morning . . . we'll see.'

It was what Beck would have done if he'd been stranded in the desert: travel by night, sleep during the day. And this was very like being in the desert, except that the desert was made of sand, not salt water. It was an inhospitable environment, drinking water was very scarce, and when the sun came up it could boil the brains of anyone caught in its glare.

He held the canvas cover up and looked thoughtfully at it. They could make an awning with this – something to shelter them from the sun, which would allow them to keep going during the day too.

'Sounds like a plan,' Farrell agreed wryly. He didn't bother asking if there was any disagreement from the others. 'Here's how we'll do it. Two of us will row, one of us will be on the tiller to steer, one of us sleeps in the bow. Every hour, we move along and swap places. Beck and I will start on the oars since we're here already. James, you're the helmsman. Miss Blake, try and get some sleep.'

Beck saw the sense of the captain's plan. The rowing would always be the hardest work. This way, after an hour each rower got a rest, either sitting at the tiller or dozing in the bow. After that rest they went back to the oars.

'And . . .' he began, then looked at Farrell for permission to speak. The captain nodded. 'Every hour we get a sip of water. Starting now.'

They solemnly passed the water bag around, and James and Abby took up their positions. Beck took hold of his oar once more and glanced resignedly at Farrell. And then, because there was nothing else to say or do, they started rowing.

Beck and Farrell quickly fell into a rhythm, pulling together, though Beck suspected that Farrell was deliberately holding back. The captain was a grown man and much the stronger of the two. If they had both put their full strength into it, Farrell's side of the boat would move faster than Beck's and they would end up going round in circles.

Beck pointed out the North Star to their helmsman, and explained where it should be in relation to the boat if they wanted to head due west. James soon got the hang of it, though it took him a while to get used to the fact that to go left you pushed the tiller to the right, and vice versa.

The boat, wobbling slightly in its course, moved on into the night.

Beck knew it was pure imagination, but it almost seemed like he could feel the weight of Steven behind him, lying on the floor of the boat. Of course, Steven weighed just as much whether he was awake or asleep. Beck wished he would moan, twitch . . . do something to show that he was still alive. If he listened closely, he could hear Steven's ragged breathing, but the splash of the oars and the sound of the waves usually drowned it out.

Steven was the one who had wanted him on this

cruise, Beck thought wryly as he pulled on his oar. He had wanted him to talk about survival. It looked like he was going to get a practical demonstration. It actually made him smile, a little.

But that was all he could find to smile about.

CHAPTER 20

A hand on Beck's shoulder shook him awake.

'Sun's coming up and you're on rowing duty,' James said. Beck sat up and looked around.

The waves had grown choppier during the night, but the boat rode them smoothly. When they reached the top of each swell, Beck reckoned he could see maybe a kilometre towards the east, where the sun was rising. Less towards the west, where it was still dark. When the boat slid down into the troughs, he was staring at a slope of water only a metre away.

There was still no sign of any other vessels.

'Also, I checked on your friend,' the older boy added. His eyes were wide and worried. 'Still no change.'

'Uh-huh.'

Beck felt for the pulse in Steven's neck, where the artery beat against the tendon. It was weak and fluttering, not strong and healthy. It didn't look like he had moved at all during the night. Beck put his ear to the man's mouth. Last night Steven's hoarse breathing had been audible from the other end of the boat. Now he could barely hear it, a few centimetres away.

Beck squatted on his haunches and gazed down at the man. There was no question that he had got worse. Last night Beck had thought there might be internal bleeding in his skull. Now he was sure of it. Steven badly needed to get to a hospital.

A gull flew overhead. He tracked it idly with his eyes, and then his attention was caught five kilometres above him by the white trails of airliners flying to or from America. *Any one of them could radio for help*, he thought – *if somehow they could be made to notice the small boat thousands of metres below them* . . . It wasn't going to happen.

Beck climbed slowly to his feet. He braced himself against the rocking of the boat and felt his joints ache. His muscles were aching from two hours of rowing the previous night, with an hour at the tiller in between. The sun was still low. Another hour or so and it would be properly up. Another hour after that and the day would start to get seriously warm. He needed to start thinking about the canvas covering. There had to be something to support it above them. They could hold it up with the oars, but then, what would we row with?

'Breakfast, Day One,' Farrell announced, breaking into Beck's thoughts. 'And to celebrate, we each get a biscuit along with our water ration.'

'And another seasick pill,' Beck ordered. He looked around the boat. Farrell, the seasoned sailor, looked OK. His face was its usual colour beneath a day's growth of stubble. But James and Abby looked distinctly pale. And even his own stomach, which he knew was pretty strong, was feeling light – as if it might suddenly decide to detach from under his ribs and float away. 'Also,' he advised, 'try and keep your eyes on the horizon. It's a steady point and it helps to settle your insides down.'

They each drank from the water bag. The small

sip made Beck's body crave more, and it took all his self-control to stop and hand it on. The water was going down – and all that remained was a little over a litre. Beck worried about how long that would last. In the heat of the day, even under cover, they would need a lot more water than that.

He knelt down beside Steven and positioned the spout over the man's mouth. Steven's head moved a little and he spluttered when the few drops of water hit his lips, but Beck was reasonably certain it went in.

'Do you need to give him quite so much?' Abby asked. Beck, the captain and James all stared at her.

'How can you ask that?' Farrell demanded – exactly what Beck was thinking. How *could* she? Steven was unconscious, but he needed water just as much as any of them.

Abby shrugged. 'I just mean, we've not got much to go round as it is. None of us wants to be here, but . . .'

'I'll try and catch us some fish later,' Beck promised, to change the subject. None of them had fully managed to adapt to their new circumstances.

They were all stressed and liable to say things they wouldn't normally. There was no point in getting worked up.

The group had to hang together, not fall apart.

A gull landed on the point of the bow with a great flapping of wings, and promptly poo'ed on the deck.

'How lovely,' Abby said, in a way that showed how *un*lovely she thought it was. The gull stared at them with yellow eyes. 'Such a nice bird,' she added.

The gull let out a harsh, wailing cry and flew off again.

Beck shook his head. 'You can eat gulls – but only if you really have to. They're tough and salty, and when you think about what *they* eat—' And then he groaned out loud, wondering how he could have been so *stupid*. Why hadn't he realized when he saw the first gull?

'They stay close to land!' he exclaimed. 'Everyone, look out for all the gulls. Which way are they flying?'

Immediately everyone was on their feet. They

held onto the sides of the boat for balance and craned their necks, looking up and around.

'There's one . . .'

'And there . . .'

Eventually they spotted maybe six . . . seven . . . eight? It was hard to say – the gulls circled and moved quickly.

'It's first light,' Beck said, 'so they're hunting for fish. That means they've flown away from land. Try to work out the average direction they've come from.'

'It's that way,' Abby said eventually, pointing. Beck, James and Farrell agreed.

'We need a bearing,' said Farrell. They couldn't just aim at a point on the horizon. There was nothing to tell one bit from the next, and the waves were knocking the boat about. They had to have a fixed direction to steer in.

Beck held up his left wrist and peered across the face of his watch towards the sun.

'I'm sorry, Beck, do you have an urgent appointment?' Abby asked, seeming confused by Beck looking at his watch.

'He's getting a bearing, Mum,' James said

impatiently. 'You point the hour hand at the sun, and north is halfway between the hour hand and twelve.'

That was exactly what Beck was doing, and he was pleased to find that James already knew this lesson.

'So that way's north.' He pointed his hand with a chopping motion. 'Which means' – he took another look at the birds – 'we need to row south-southwest.'

CHAPTER 21

The sea became even rougher as they rowed. The peaks of the waves now broke into small splashes of white water before falling down again. It was not the kind of sea on which Beck wanted to be adrift in a lifeboat.

The sun had risen further and its light spread further to the west. The day was warming, to the point where Beck knew they would have to think about putting the cover up before much longer. Then another wave carried the lifeboat up a little bit higher, and James called: 'There's an island!'

Beck and the captain had their backs to it because they were rowing. Beck squinted over his shoulder and caught a glimpse the next time the sea lifted the boat up. The island was a dark smudge between sea and sky.

They got a better view as they drew nearer. It wasn't large – no more than a kilometre long, as far as he could see. There was no high ground on it – no hills, no cliffs – and as they approached, they realized that it was surrounded by a strip of dirty sand. Above this was a small forest of scrubby palm trees and bushes. The waves broke against the shore with a ferocious roar, dissolving into plumes of white spray and foam.

'There's rocks or a reef around it,' said Farrell. 'Those waves wouldn't break like that on their own. We need to find the right way in . . .'

Abby was on the tiller. James, in the bow, strained his eyes to spot a likely landing place. They had to row three quarters of the way around the island before they found a spot the captain was happy with. The waves still broke there, but it seemed to Beck that they were smoother, running cleanly up the beach. The boat should be able to run up with them and then touch down gently on the sand. But it would still be a rough ride in.

'Everyone, get a lifejacket on,' Farrell ordered. 'Miss Blake, fit one onto Steven. Just in case we all get tipped in.'

There was a bustle of activity for a minute or two while everyone did as they were told. Abby took twice as long as she needed to with Steven. Her face was set and her lips pursed as she tried not to touch the blood that still matted his hair. Eventually Beck got down to help her.

Farrell waited until everyone was ready.

'James, the moment we hit the sand, I want you out and holding onto the boat, OK? Drag us as far up the beach as you can. We'll be right behind you.'

'Sure!' James nodded and bared his teeth in a grin. He actually looked like he might be enjoying this. Beck had found out before that even the most hardened loners could thrive as part of a team – especially if they were on a survival mission. If every-one played to their strengths, and was encouraged and supported, then the whole team's morale could be incredible despite the danger.

James stood poised in the bow. Abby aimed the boat dead on to the shore, and Farrell and Beck heaved together. The boat surged ahead, riding the wave towards the island like a professional surfer.

Suddenly James was shouting and pointing ahead. 'I think there's a rock . . .'

Beck looked over his shoulder and just caught a glimpse of it. It had been hidden by the surf; it wasn't big enough to be seen from a distance – just a lump sticking out of the sea – but it would do some real damage and it was dead ahead of them.

Farrell had seen it as well, but too late. He was just opening his mouth to shout an instruction to Abby to steer away when they hit it.

James was flung over the bow into the water as the boat stopped dead. There was a crunch and the sound of splintering fibreglass. Water gushed into it through a crack that was well over a metre long.

The boat lurched, and was now sideways on to the island and the breaking waves. A wall of water rose above it and tipped the small boat so steeply that Beck was plunged into the sea after James.

CHAPTER 22

Bubbles and water surged around Beck and he felt himself being thrown onto the sand. He pushed his feet down and fought his way upright. He broke the surface, gasping for breath, eyes stinging from the salt, just in time to see the boat poised to topple on top of him. Abby and Farrell were clinging on for dear life. Steven's still form was being flung about like a rag doll.

But slowly the boat fell back the other way, righting itself and half full of water. Beck rushed forward to grab hold of one of the life ropes, and heaved on it.

'Come on!' he shouted over his shoulder. James came splashing forward to help him. Maybe things hadn't quite gone to plan, but they still needed to get the boat up onto the beach. Farrell leaped out and joined them. Between them they heaved, muscles straining, and dragged the boat as far as they could.

It still floated, just, so that every time a wave came in they were able to drag it a bit further. But it was gradually sinking because of the crack in the hull, and rose a little less with each wave. Finally it was as far up the beach as they could get it. The waves reached the stern but not the bow. And now water ran out of the crack rather than in.

Abby waited expectantly, obviously assuming that someone would help her out onto the beach.

Instead Farrell clambered in and heaved Steven up in his arms. 'Boys, I'm going to pass him to you . . .'

Abby pursed her lips but stepped daintily down on her own.

James and Beck were considerably less dainty as they took Steven's weight. The collar of his life-jacket supported his head as they staggered up the beach and laid him down on the sand. Beck knelt to check that the bandage was still secure.

Meanwhile Farrell rummaged in the boat and

passed Abby the first-aid box and the emergency flares. He took the rations box and water himself and jumped down onto the sand.

The drama must have given them all an energy rush; now that they were safe on dry land, Beck suddenly realized how tired he was. Everyone looked ready to drop on the sand, there and then.

'Not yet.' Beck was firm. 'Further up the beach – look, there.'

There were about twenty metres of beach between the sea and the trees. The sand was smooth and damp for about half of that. At the top edge of the damp bit was a line of dead seaweed and bits of wood. These collected at the high-water mark – the point where the sea reached when the tide was at its highest.

At the edge of the trees, a large boulder stuck out of the sand. It was above the tide mark, and sand was piled slightly higher on one side than the other. This meant that Beck could see which side faced the wind and which side would provide shelter. They could rest there.

They made a sad, bedraggled group as they

trudged up the beach. Two adults and two boys, carrying an unconscious man between them, all of them soaking wet. At last they reached the shelter of the boulder, where they laid Steven down and dropped to the ground themselves. Huddled together, hugging their knees for warmth, they watched the sun come up properly.

We can't sit here for ever, Beck told himself, *but I'll give it five minutes, just to rest and get our bearings . . .*

'When will someone come looking for us?' he asked.

Farrell shook his head. 'They'll miss our regular check-in, so pretty soon they'll realize something's wrong. They'll launch an air-sea search . . . in the area where we were supposed to be. They'll follow the course we should have taken all the way from Miami. But we were so far off course . . .' He let his voice trail away.

'Will they find the wreck of the ship?' James asked.

'No hope. That beauty has sunk to the bottom without trace. And God only knows how deep that water is. That lifeboat there, and us, may be all that's left for anyone to find . . .' The captain's eyes lingered on the stranded boat, though he didn't seem to be looking at it. Beck wondered if their thoughts were heading in the same direction. Now that the drama of the shipwreck was over, now that they were on solid ground, they could spare the time to ask the question: *What the heck happened?*

Beck finally said what he had known from the start: 'Someone sank the ship deliberately, and they didn't care that we were still on it. The crew just left us. Why?' He looked from Farrell's face to Abby's – not expecting them to know the answer, just to emphasize that he meant it. The captain's features were sunken and hollow, like a close friend had just died. Abby just looked weary.

'I have no idea,' said Farrell quietly.

And that was all the answer he was going to get for now, Beck thought. Maybe they would never know.

What he *did* know was that they were stranded with no means of escape, no way of communicating with the mainland, and no supplies apart from a first-aid box, half a packet of biscuits and a half-empty bag of water.

Beck gave the lifeboat another glance. Later, he thought, they could turn it upside down and use it as a shelter. Protection from the sun during the day, warmth at night. He assumed they would be there at night.

And from what Farrell was saying, they could be here for quite some time.

That reminded him. Hadn't there been a tropical storm brewing nearby? It had been to the southeast when he saw it on the radar the previous day. And it had had hurricane warning flags attached to it.

He looked in that direction now and could make out an ominous gathering of dark clouds on the distant horizon. The clouds rose high into the air, shaped like a giant's anvil. Cumulonimbus. Beck recognized those instantly and he knew what they meant.

A storm. And a big one. It was some way off, which was some relief.

For now.

This island was no more than three or four

metres above the water, at its highest point, unless you climbed a tree.

Beck knew that if a hurricane struck here, it would not be a nice place to be. Not at all nice.

'But look on the bright side!' Abby piped up suddenly, her mood changing so quickly that Beck looked round in surprise. 'We've got survival expert Beck Granger with us!' she continued. 'He'll save us, right? So, Beck, go on, tell us what to do!'

CHAPTER 23

'OK,' Beck said half an hour later, 'here goes . . .'

They had collected all the leaves and pieces of wood they could carry, and piled them on a flat rocky ledge at the top of the beach. The centre of the island was thick with undergrowth, so Beck had made everyone burrow right into the bushes and scrub for the deadest, driest items they could find. Stuff that would burn very nicely.

They were going to make two fires – both would act as signal fires: the first would be all prepped and ready to be lit if they spotted a plane or passing ship by day; and the other fire would be to light now, to keep them visible by day but also through the night. At night, especially, it would act as a bright beacon shining out through the darkness.

At the core of both fires was a pile of dry leaves and twigs. The outer layers were made of thicker and thicker bits of wood. Some were already the right length; some had had to be snapped and broken down. The core, the kindling, would catch first. The bigger pieces would keep the fires going.

On the big signal fire, which would remain unlit until needed, they would lay big green palm branches that, in turn, would produce large amounts of smoke when they burned.

That was the important part.

Smoke is more visible by day than flame.

The ledge was flat, and a boulder sheltered it from the prevailing wind. Beck wanted to be able to sit around their night fire while also sheltered by the wind. Nor did he want it to burn too fast in the breeze.

Beck knelt down by the pile.

'I don't suppose you've got matches?' Abby asked.

He felt his bare throat again. The thought of his missing fire steel made him bite his lip. He saw

James look questioningly at him – he'd obviously remembered the steel too.

'No,' he said shortly, 'I haven't.'

He was going to have to use an alternative method, and he knew it would give his hands blisters.

Well, you will have to live with that, Beck Granger, he told himself. *Consider it a lesson learned. Never leave your fire steel behind again*.

'Mum, he's probably going to make a fire drill,' James explained. 'He'll spin it with a bow—'

'Um, well almost,' Beck interrupted quietly. 'Right idea, but . . .'

A drill and bow would have been Plan B, since Beck didn't have his fire steel. The last time he had made a fire with the drill-and-bow method had been with Peter when they were in the Sahara. The bow was a curved piece of wood with a string joining both ends. The drill was a short, pointed length of wood. You twined the string around the drill and moved the bow back and forth, making it spin. You used a small block of wood in one hand to press down on the spinning drill. This creates friction at the drill's base; and friction means heat, smoke and eventually a small ember.

But he was going to have to resort to Plan C.

'You need string to make a bow,' he said, 'and we don't have any. So I'm using my hands . . .'

Beck picked his way through the sticks and twigs until he found what he wanted.

First, he found his drill. It was as long and straight as he could find. It looked like the kind of thing you would kill vampires with – two foot long and not much thicker than a pen. And with a blunt point. He wished he had a knife to smooth off the shaft of the stick a bit more, but it would have to do. The rougher it was, the worse the blisters would be. Beck knew that.

He then got his base plate by using a stick to pry a slab of bark off a tree. It was about the size of a tea plate.

The pile of kindling on the rock next to the piled-up wood was like a small bird's nest, a mini mound of dried leaves and twigs. He put the base plate down next to it and knelt beside it.

'James, I need you to help me with this.'

James knelt down opposite him and Beck held the plate firm against the ground with one foot. Beck spat into his palms, then held them flat together with the drill between them, the tip pressed into the plate. Then, with a slow, smooth, easy motion, he began to move his hands. Back and forth, starting from the top of the spindle and slowly working his way down to the bottom.

'Your turn, James,' Beck said urgently. 'We take it in turns, alternately, so the spindle is continually spinning. OK?'

The drill spun fast with each movement, and the boys worked the drill, keeping it spinning. All the time it was building up friction and heat at its base.

'It's going to take a while . . .' Beck warned.

'Here, let me help too,' Farrell said suddenly. He crouched down next to Beck and James to join the rota. 'My hands are bigger and tougher – together we can do this.'

And so Beck let him join in. James soon got tired, and instead helped to hold the base plate in position, and Beck and Farrell kept working the spindle.

The captain could make the drill spin twice as

fast as Beck could. Back and forth, back and forth . . .

'Keep it pressed into the plate,' Beck spluttered between breaths. Both he and Farrell were sweating hard.

Farrell just grunted and kept going.

'There's smoke!' James cried at last. Beck didn't know how long they had been going, but James was right. There it was – the tiniest wisp of smoke at the drill's tip.

'Keep going,' Beck said grimly. More and more smoke accumulated, and a very faint smell of burning wood reached his nostrils.

Beck and the captain kept at it until the tip was almost obscured by a small cloud of smoke hanging in the air around it. The top layer of the base plate around the tip had turned into a very fine layer of scorched wood dust that glowed with heat.

'And stop,' Beck whispered.

Farrell broke off immediately with a sigh of relief, cradling his hands under his arms.

Beck very gently tipped the dust into the bird's nest of tinder that he had prepared earlier. The dust glowed a dull red and started to fade. Beck pursed his lips and gently blew onto it. The red glow came back, wavered, went dark, came back again. This time it stayed. And then it started to spread, moving from the powder and into the tinder.

The fresh smell of burning wood grew stronger, and thin tendrils of smoke started to drift up into the air.

Beck gently pushed the small pile across the rocky ledge and into the base of the main fire. He kept blowing at it until suddenly the flames burst out of the small tinder bundle. The fire had caught.

The others gathered around gratefully. The sun and the wind had helped dry them off after their rough landing, but there was a clinging chill inside each of them that needed a good fire.

Beck waited a couple of minutes for the fire to spread through the pile. Then he gathered a handful of younger, less dry leaves and dumped them on top. Immediately grey smoke began to billow from the fire, mingled with the flames. Before long, he thought, it should be visible for miles.

'That should attract attention, right?' James was

almost glowing with pride. Beck understood. He had experienced those feelings many times before. He knew that his fire would help them survive – and in some way James had made that happen.

'You bet, buddy,' Beck agreed. He couldn't argue. It would certainly attract attention – if there was anyone about to see it.

But with a hurricane on its way, would anyone still be around?

CHAPTER 24

'So, next,' Beck said, 'we look for water.'

'Or how about some food?' Abby asked. 'You can catch us that fish and we can cook it on our lovely fire.'

Beck shook his head. They could survive for days, even weeks, without food after they'd eaten the ration biscuits from the lifeboat. Lack of water could finish them off in a fraction of that time.

'*Water*,' he and James said together. They looked at each other in surprise. Beck tipped his head to indicate that James should go ahead.

James grinned. 'You should have read that magazine article about Beck more closely, Mum. He said that the human body is seventy-five per cent water. Even if you lose just five per cent of that, then you start to deteriorate, big time.'

Now Beck came to think of it, he remembered giving that interview. The reporter had loved hearing the gruesome descriptions. Heart rate and body temperature shoot up, muscles cramp, fatigue knocks you out and your body shuts down.

Back on the ship, Beck doubted James would ever have spoken to his mother like that. That was before he had started to feel part of the team. Beck liked the change. He was pretty sure Abby didn't. She gave her son a sideways look.

'There might already be some water on the island,' she pointed out.

'There might,' Beck agreed. 'But there might not, and if there isn't, then we need to start thinking smart.'

He looked over at their small pile of possessions. It wasn't much. The first-aid box, the biscuits, the bag of water, the boat's canvas cover, and the tin box with the flares in it. Beck's eyes settled back on the first-aid box – just what he needed. He tipped the contents into a neat pile.

'Now I need some fabric – something good and absorbent . . .'

He ran his eyes over each of them in turn, and looked down at himself. He wasn't going to ask Abby to undress, so that left him, James and Farrell. They all wore cotton T-shirts, but the captain's was twice the size of the ones the two boys wore. Beck could also see that he still had his vest on underneath, which would at least give him some protection from the sun.

'Captain, I, uh, need to borrow your T-shirt . . .'

Farrell's eyebrows shot up, but he peeled it off and handed it over without comment. Beck hurried down to the water's edge with the empty first-aid box and filled it to the brim. Coming back to the others, he laid it on the ground and stretched the captain's T-shirt over the top. He tied the shirt in place with a strip of bandage around the edge of the box, and laid it on a flat piece of sand where the sun would fall right onto it.

'I'm sure we'll get some water at the end of this,' Abby said, 'but I've no idea how.'

'He's making a salt-water still, Mum,' James said

impatiently. All eyes turned to him and he flushed. 'We can't drink salt water,' he explained. 'It just dehydrates us even more. This way, the sun will evaporate the salt water in the box. It turns to steam but the salt stays in the box. The steam soaks into the shirt, and it's fresh, so we can drink it, uh, somehow . . .' He trailed off.

Beck was impressed: James had obviously done a lot of reading up on survival skills. He finished for him. 'We wring the shirt out into here to collect the water.'

He opened the tin box. It still had the two flares in it: thin metal tubes about twenty centimetres long, with a pull-tab at one end to fire them. He tucked one into his pocket and tried to stick the other one in too, but there wasn't room. He passed the second flare to the nearest person, who was Abby.

'Could you hold onto that, please? Thanks. Captain, it's your shirt – could you be in charge of wringing it out?'

Farrell smiled for the first time since the ship had sunk, and saluted. 'Aye aye, sir.'

'Next . . .' Beck looked from Abby, to James, and

back. There were two more jobs he could think of that needed doing. He could do one of them and he knew who he would prefer to have with him.

'Miss Blake, please could you be in charge of marking out a nice big "SOS" on the sand?'

'And what do I do for the other twenty-three hours and fifty-five minutes of my day?'

Beck smothered a smile. 'It will take you more than five minutes to do it properly. From a plane, the letters will look tiny. They need to be five, six metres high at least. Mark them in the sand, but also use sticks, rocks . . . anything you can find. And keep them above the high-water mark so that the tide doesn't just wash them away when it comes in.'

'Nice and big. Sticks and rocks. Got it.'

'And keep an eye on Steven,' Beck added. 'Keep on giving him water from the bag. Meanwhile, James and I will explore the island.'

CHAPTER 25

'I can't believe you were just telling my mum what to do.' James looked at Beck with respect as they clambered over a fallen tree trunk. The centre of the island was a dense cluster of trees and bushes. They were out of sight of the sea, though they could still hear the sound of waves breaking.

'If we're all going to survive,' Beck said with a shrug, 'we have to do it together. Everyone has to do something. We can't carry passengers.'

And he couldn't deny that, deep down, he had enjoyed giving instructions to Abby Blake. He had guessed that being told what to do by anyone was a rare experience for her, and James had just confirmed it.

'Yeah, but . . . Never mind.' James stopped and

his gaze ran up a palm tree in front of them. 'Hey, look – coconuts!'

Beck followed where he was staring. The palm tree rose up a good ten metres or so and, sure enough, there was a cluster of them at the top, where the leaves emerged. They were the size of footballs and green, each one wrapped in a layer of leaf.

'That's cool.' Beck was very pleased to see them. They couldn't live off coconuts for ever, but the flesh inside the shell was nutritious and the coconut milk was refreshing and hydrating. 'We'll gather some up later. For the time being we're just looking for water.'

'Do you think there's any animal life here? Apart from us?'

Beck stopped and rested his hands on his hips. His gaze travelled slowly over the tightly packed bushes. 'To be honest, I doubt there's anything larger than an insect around here.'

The island was uninhabited. He was certain of that. The trees and bushes were too dense. There were no natural pathways because no one, human or animal, had pushed a way through them before.

But there would be insects. They got everywhere.

'Yeah? I had French-fried caterpillars in Mexico once. They were pretty good,' James stated.

'Cool! Well, maybe we can find some caterpillars to French-fry,' Beck said with a smile. James didn't get squirmy over eating insects: that was another good sign. Other people would, and Beck was prepared to bet that James's mother was one of them.

It would still be nicer to eat fish, or maybe crabs. He could get them from the shoreline. They would have to cook them, because though fish is OK to eat raw, raw crab can be toxic.

But water was the main thing at the moment. He knew they would struggle to collect enough evaporated sea water to live off. If they could find a spring – even a pool that wasn't stagnant – that would be perfect.

James kicked his heel at the ground. The earth was a dirty mixture of sand and pebbles.

'There has to be water down here or the trees wouldn't be growing. The roots must be reaching down to water underground.'

'True, but it might be a long way down. If we dig a well, then water will soak into it – eventually – but we might not get enough back to make it worthwhile.'

James's face fell, but he recovered in a moment. Beck was pleased to see him making the decision to be cheerful. You needed a good mental attitude to keep one step ahead of what life threw at you. James had probably read that in the magazine too.

'So, what were you doing in Mexico?' Beck asked, making conversation as they pushed their way further through the undergrowth.

James shrugged. 'Oh, you know . . .' Beck didn't. 'Kind of . . . work experience. For the family firm. In fact that's pretty much all I do when I'm not at school. Not a lot of time for anything else.'

Beck thought of his friend Peter again. He was still sure that Peter would get on well with this boy. They would be able to talk to each other for hours. But Peter also played cricket, loved swimming, and was also pretty musical . . . The thought of spending your entire teens just doing work experience was a bit depressing.

'Yeah, well . . .' James shrugged. 'Granddad's kind of determined. So, anyway, how about you? What do you do with your time?'

It was a pretty obvious way of changing the subject, but Beck thought it was a probably a fair question.

'Me? I . . . uh . . . I . . . uh . . .'

'Apart from have adventures, that is,' James said. He added a grin to show it was a friendly question, not a dig.

'Hey, I don't get into them deliberately!' Beck protested. And then he stopped. Actually, he reckoned, that wasn't quite true. Yes, quite a few of his adventures had been accidents – but he had only been able to survive because when he was younger he had gone out of his way to learn the skills of indigenous people around the world. It hadn't been an accident that he had learned so much. All those things had happened to him because he had sought them out.

'I guess . . . yeah, I guess it's work experience too!' Beck had never really thought about it like that before. He had certainly never put it into words. But suddenly, at that moment, he knew what he wanted to do with his life. 'I want to put it all into practice. In a few years I want to work for Green Force. Like my mum and dad did.'

'Your mum and dad . . .' James pulled a face, and for a while they trudged along in silence.

Beck was used to this: people hear about your parents being dead and suddenly don't know what to say.

'It's OK,' he said gently. 'I mean, it's not OK – it sucks as big as anything can suck – but I'm OK with it. Even though I really miss them. Especially at family times – you know, like Christmas.'

It was always a struggle, and Beck knew it affected Al too, though he never admitted it. Al had lost a brother and a dear friend when Beck's parents died. No matter how much fun they tried to have with all the celebrations and parties, sooner or later their thoughts would always return to the two empty spaces in their hearts.

James seemed quite happy that the subject had changed.

'Yeah, Christmas! We'll be staying in Miami—'

Then, unexpectedly, he laughed. 'Has it occurred to you that we're both going into the family firm?'

It wasn't long before Beck was pretty sure that the waves he heard ahead of him were closer than the ones behind. They were already more than halfway across the island.

Several times, Beck dropped to his knees to study the roots of a tree or bush. They all disappeared into the sandy mixture that passed for earth in this place, but there was never any that looked darker than the rest. That meant that there was no water close to the surface.

There was plenty of fallen wood. They stopped at a tree that had fallen across their way, and Beck used a stick to pry back chunks of bark. He wasn't going to use his bare hands in a tropical climate, where things with sharp, poisonous teeth or stings might lurk under any bit of wood, and even a scratch could quickly go septic. He wished he had a decent knife – or, even better, a machete.

Several pale, wriggling insect grubs tumbled out

and writhed away from the light. He let one drop into his hand and held it up for inspection.

It wasn't a type he recognized, but it felt plump between his fingers. A few of these in anyone's stomach would stop them going hungry. He held it out to James.

'What do you think?'

'Um . . .' James wrinkled his brow, obviously trying to remember the survival tips he had read. 'They're not furry, so that's good.'

'Right,' Beck agreed. Fur on an insect was always bad news. It was probably poisonous, and even if it wasn't, then it was designed to get under the skin of any predators and itch like mad, maybe leading to infection. So you didn't want that in your mouth and going down your throat.

'And there's no black dots.'

James meant black patches that showed through the skin – another sign that the grub was very bad for eating.

'So . . .' He suddenly looked a lot less enthusiastic as he realized what he was saying. This wasn't French-fried. It wasn't served up with lots of spices. It was a raw, live insect. 'It's probably OK . . .'

'Almost certainly,' Beck agreed, popping it into his mouth. He crunched it between his teeth and felt the insides spurt onto his tongue. The little creature's insides had the consistency of snot, and it had spent all its life on a diet of wood, so that was what it tasted like. Wood-flavoured snot. It wasn't the greatest taste in the world, but it wasn't the worst.

Beck held another one out for James. 'Give it a go? Just think of it as French-fried caterpillars, without the French-frying.'

James's mouth twisted as he studied the thing between Beck's fingers. All the things he had read about were turning into actual reality. It was quite a leap to make, but he took the grub, popped it into his mouth and swallowed, all at once.

'It wriggles all the way down,' he gasped.

'You're meant to bite on it first.'

James still looked as if he was about to bring it back up again, but the urge soon passed. He gave an uncertain smile, as if he was amazed at himself.

'I think it's gone . . . OK, that wasn't too bad . . .'

He was looking at the ground. Suddenly he let

out a whoop and slipped his hand under a shrub.

'French-fried caterpillar coming up!' he proclaimed, and proudly brandished one of the largest centipedes Beck had ever seen. It was a good thirty centimetres long and as thick as a banana. The segments of its body were each at least one or two centimetres across. They glistened a silvery blue, like polished steel. The creature looked like it had been built in a factory rather than hatched. It writhed in James's grasp, stubby legs waving helplessly.

Beck's eyes went wide. 'Put it down, quick!' he shouted – but too late. The giant centipede brought its head round and struck out at James's hand.

CHAPTER 26

James screamed and dropped the creature. He stared in horror at the red mark blossoming on his skin.

'Ow! Owowowowow! It *hurts*!'

'Let's see,' Beck said.

James held out his hand. The creature had bitten him on the tip of his middle right finger. It was the finger on which he wore the silver ring Beck had noticed when they first met.

'What was it?' James whimpered.

Beck shot the giant centipede a look. It was slinking away into the undergrowth. He wondered if it was pleased with itself for teaching the giant mammal a lesson.

'Scolopendra, I think.'

'Poisonous?'

'Yup.' James looked like he was about to faint. 'But almost never fatal,' Beck added hastily.

James snatched his hand away. 'What do you mean, almost?' he yelped.

Beck grabbed the hand back and peered closely at the bite. It was just a red mark, a dot with an inflamed edge. 'Almost never, to humans. Not unless you've got a weak heart.'

He screwed up his face, trying to remember. He and Al had been in a camp in Belize, and there had been a talk on local wildlife. Scolopendra had been one of the things the guy mentioned. Their venom was cardiotoxic, which meant that it attacked the heart. But there wasn't enough of it to kill anything bigger than a rodent. Humans would just suffer pain. Quite a lot of it.

'Symptoms are local pain . . .'

'Got that.'

'Swelling . . .'

James studied his finger dubiously.

'There might be a bit of fever – though probably not in your case, it was only a small bite . . .'

'Didn't feel small.'

Beck grinned. 'And a strange urge to run around screaming, "Aargh, aargh, giant centipede, aargh!"'

James smiled, very weakly. 'I think I've got all of those.'

'You want to see one hunting down a rat,' Beck said. The guy in Belize had showed a film of one doing just that. It had chased, killed, and then eaten the poor animal. It sent shivers down your spine. It just wasn't the kind of thing you thought a centipede should be able to do.

'You know, I *really* don't—'

'Look, have you got a hanky on you?'

'Uh, yeah . . .'

'OK, we'll use that as a temporary bandage. Then we'll go back to the camp and wash the bite, put a bandage on – that's about all we can do for now. You'll be OK. But take that ring off. Your finger will probably swell up and that could be a lot more uncomfortable.'

James looked reluctant for a moment. Beck remembered that the ring was a family heirloom – maybe James was worried about losing it. But he was obviously more worried about losing a finger, because he tugged it off and passed it to Beck. Beck held it lightly in his fingers while James rummaged single-handed in his pockets.

The outside of the ring was smooth, but there were letters carved around the inside. Beck held it up and squinted at the tiny writing.

It was a series of single words.

MASTERY. OBEDIENCE. SUCCESS. LOGIC. UNDERSTANDING.

'Hey!' James had produced a hanky, but now he saw what Beck was doing and snatched the ring back. 'Mind your own business!'

'Gee, sorry.' Beck blinked in surprise at the sudden change in mood. He realized he had been sticking his nose in – it wasn't any of his business what those words were. Supposing it was some private message – like from a loved one. But he also thought that James was over-reacting a little.

James must have thought so too because he gave a nervous little laugh. 'Sorry. It's just . . .' He trailed off.

'Family heirloom, right?' Beck bent his head to tie the handkerchief around James's finger.

'Yeah.' James forced another weak smile, and held the ring up again. 'It's kind of the family motto. My grandfather founded the family business and he says these are the qualities he expects us all to have. If everyone in the business has all these, then there's nothing we can't do . . . He says.'

Beck had finished tying the makeshift bandage. 'You don't sound convinced.'

James pulled a face. 'Like I said before, Granddad expects me to go into the business too, but . . .' He shrugged and looked around. 'There's more to life than just making money. I never really thought about it until . . . you know. We almost died on that ship!'

'Uh-huh.' Beck could certainly agree that there was nothing like almost dying to make you realize just how great and valuable life was.

'I mean, look at what you do,' James went on. 'All the things you've seen. The world's so . . . so *amazing*. Even somewhere like here – this stupid dumpsville island that's crawling with giant poisonous centipedes. Humans could just vanish and the world would carry on, because it's made that way – all the ecosystems just work together . . . who would want to spoil all that?'

Beck raised an eyebrow. He didn't quite follow James's little speech. James had started by talking about money, then somehow he had got on to life, and what a beautiful world it was, and protecting the environment. Beck agreed with him on both counts, but he wasn't quite sure how it all linked together in James's head.

But it was none of his business, and right now there were more important things to worry about.

'I'll look after the ring for you, shall I? I've got a pocket with a zip.' James nodded mutely and so Beck slipped it into his pocket. 'Let's get back to the camp.'

They took a slightly different route back, to widen their search. But there was still no sign of water. The effort of walking around the island, pushing through the thick foliage, had made Beck thirsty. Their water supply was going to be a real issue.

James seemed to be reading his thoughts. 'There was this website that you gave an interview to

'. . . you talked about solar stills. We could use the boat cover to make one of them . . .'

'Good idea,' Beck agreed. James was obviously one of those people who was able to turn all his knowledge into something that was useful in the real world.

They could dig a pit and lay the cover over it, weighing it down with rocks. Dampness from the ground would collect on the underside of the cover. If they put the tin box underneath the middle of the cover and weighted the this point down with a rock, that would make a slope. Droplets of water would run down it and drip into the box.

'I remember that website,' Beck said. They had come to the edge of the trees and emerged onto the beach. They were some way from the camp, so they turned right and walked along the edge of the sand. 'They left out a detail – they said it was too much for their young readers . . .'

'Yeah?' James's eyes were wide and Beck grinned.

'You can increase the amount of water that evaporates by putting damp stuff into the hole. You know, vegetation . . . or just peeing into it.'

'Oh, gross.' Then James laughed. 'So – whenever we want to go, we go in the hole?'

'Well, yeah. All the impurities would be left behind when it evaporated.'

James shook as he tried to subdue his mirth. 'Including . . . including *my mum*?'

The thought of the high-and-mighty, elegant Abby doing that was enough to make Beck start laughing too. They were still laughing together when they reached the camp.

The first thing Beck noticed was that Abby had not marked out the SOS in the sand. There were some scuff marks that might have been the top half of the first 'S', but that was all.

The second was the captain and Abby, standing side by side and looking gravely at them. Beck felt his good mood disappear like a burst bubble.

'What?' he asked.

Abby came forward and pulled him into a hug that he was too surprised to resist. 'Oh, Beck, I'm so sorry.'

She stepped back and Farrell came forward. For

a moment Beck thought the captain was going to hug him too.

'Beck, I'm very sorry – I'm afraid Steven has died from his injuries.'

CHAPTER 27

Steven lay peacefully where Beck had left him. He was in the shade of a tree, still with a lifejacket under his head. At first glance he almost looked like he could be asleep – but not if you looked closer.

Nothing looks more dead than a dead person.

A faint groan came from James. He had gone green, his eyes fixed on the body – he looked like he was about to throw up. Beck had seen dead people before; James hadn't. Beck quickly grabbed him by the shoulders and marched him over to Abby.

'James got bit on the finger,' he said sharply. 'It needs to be washed and bandaged.'

Abby immediately became one hundred per cent mum. 'Here, let me see . . .'

While they were both distracted, Beck looked at Farrell for an explanation.

The captain shook his head. 'It was very sudden. I was checking the water still while Abby was looking after him . . . She called me over, said he was going . . . He was gone by the time I got there. Beck, I don't think any of us could have helped. That bang on the head – he needed help. It wasn't our fault.'

'It was the fault of whoever sank the ship,' Beck said darkly. 'They murdered him.' He was surprised to feel tears pricking his eyes. It wasn't like he and Steven had been close friends. They had got along OK, but they hadn't known each other that long.

But Steven was the first person Beck had lost in a survival situation. Yes, he had seen people killed by the emergency that created the situation in the first place. A crashing plane, an exploding volcano. That had always been before he became responsible for them. But this? No one had ever gone and died on him like this.

'We'll have to bury him, Beck, and quick.'

Beck knew what the captain meant. In this heat a dead body could go off very quickly. And the gulls and crabs would smell him and come for him . . . They had to get Steven out of the way. But digging a grave would be tiring and energy consuming, and make them thirstier than ever.

Abby had come back to join them. 'I was just thinking – we all pooled what we had when we got here, but no one went through Steven's pockets, did they?'

Beck and Farrell both stared at her.

She shrugged. 'I'm sorry, but we can't afford to be sentimental, can we? Before we bury him we should find out what he has.'

She was absolutely right, but Beck wished she could have found a better time to have this bright idea. Like, *before* Steven died.

'Look, Beck, I can—' Farrell began, but Beck shook his head.

'It's OK. I'll do it.' Beck wouldn't want a complete stranger going through *his* things.

Steven was still dressed in the day clothes he had been wearing when the ship went down: trainers, trousers, leather jacket. Beck tried the trouser pockets first. 'Hanky . . . keys . . .' There was nothing in the outside pockets of Steven's jacket. Beck unzipped it and felt inside. 'Wallet.'

The wallet contained Steven's cards, driving licence, a few soaked dollar bills, and a photograph of a small girl.

Beck looked at this for a moment. No one ever died in isolation. Every person's death affected someone. He remembered Steven mentioning a daughter. Six years old.

People liked to think they would somehow magically 'know' when a loved one died. Beck knew from bitter experience that this wasn't true. Somewhere, this little girl – or another child, or Steven's own parents – were happily going about their business right now, not knowing that their lives had just been torn apart.

He shut the wallet and tried the inside pocket on the other side. His fingers closed around a piece of folded paper. It was a single A4 sheet, soggy but drying slowly. 'And this.'

'Can we use anything?' Abby asked.

Beck idly flicked the page out so that it unfolded. Its survival value was almost zero. 'Not really.

Though it might have been handy when we were starting the fire—'

He stopped, looked more closely. It was as if something on the paper had snagged his eye. Like hearing your name mentioned in a crowded room – there are things that just catch your attention. This was one of them.

The laser-printed text had blurred in the water but it was still legible. No, he hadn't been mistaken. There it was in black and white.

Lumos.

Beck's heart began to pound as he studied the page more closely. There was a logo – planet Earth, ablaze with light, and the words LUMOS INC. There was an office address for a street in Miami.

The very first line said, COMPANY CONFIDENTIAL: NOT TO BE READ BY GRADES BELOW EXECUTIVE LEVEL.

'Beck?' Farrell asked. 'You look like you've seen a ghost.'

Beck held up the paper. 'It's Lumos . . .'

The captain shrugged. 'The energy company?'

In theory, Beck knew that Lumos was just that – an energy company. It was also a company he had run into more than once, and the experience had never been good. They were greedy, they were corrupt, and they didn't care about the damage they did as long as it made money.

He also knew something about Lumos that he had never said out loud in any of his interviews. Al had told him very firmly not to. Lumos had powerful lawyers and Beck couldn't prove anything.

But he said it now.

'Lumos killed my parents.'

CHAPTER 28

'Can you prove that, Beck?' Abby asked. 'Because if you can't, that's a very dangerous thing to claim in public . . . I'm just saying.'

Beck looked her in the eye. 'Sue me.'

This piece of paper just didn't make sense, he told himself. Was Steven working for Lumos? Steven, whom Al had known and trusted for years? Would Al have trusted him to look after Beck if there had been the tiniest atom of doubt in his mind?

How the *heck* could Steven have anything to do with them?

But here was the paper, in his pocket. A very important bit of paper, apparently: confidential, only to be read by very senior people.

Something wasn't right.

'So what else does the paper say?' Abby asked. Beck glared at her for a moment. He didn't care what else the paper said. The whole point of this had been to see if Steven had anything on him they could use for survival. Instead they had found this. It meant that everything just got a whole lot more complicated – and yet again Lumos had wormed its way into his life. The corporation was like those parasitic wasps that laid eggs in other insects. When the eggs hatched, the grubs ate their host from within. Beck felt that Lumos must have laid its eggs in him long ago, and now yet another one was hatching.

The next line read: *Fuel for the Future – a Strategy for Exploitable Energy Resources in the Caribbean Basin*. There was a map on the reverse. He looked at the front again, and another phrase caught his eye in the opening paragraphs. *Methane hydrates*.

'Hey, James, weren't you talking about these?' He pointed at the line.

James peered at the text. 'Uh, yeah. Ship disappearances, and, uh, that . . . Yeah.'

'So why would Lumos be interested in ship disappearances?' Farrell asked.

Beck shrugged. He doubted whether Lumos wanted ships to disappear. Lumos would want as many ships as possible to be up and about, running their dirty, inefficient engines so that Lumos could supply them with more fuel and make more profits.

'Methane hydrate could be a really good fuel source,' James said. 'It's formed by natural gas freezing under pressure, deep down under the ground – but it's much better than natural gas, if it's handled properly.'

'What happens if it's not handled properly?' Farrell asked.

'It's better than natural gas, but it's also even more explosive. One small mistake, and – *boom!*' James mimed an explosion with his hands. 'Remember that oil rig that caught fire?'

'Deepwater Horizon?' Beck said. He remembered Al's interest in the case. Green Force's lawyers had been busy ever since. Deepwater Horizon had been an oil rig in the Gulf of Mexico that exploded in 2010. Several of the crew had been killed. The rig had blazed away until it sank two days later. The well it had been drilling had gushed oil straight into the ocean for the next three months. It was an ecological disaster.

'That was an oil well,' the captain said. 'They weren't drilling for methane hydrate.'

'No, but some people think they might have set a pocket of it off. Methane hydrate hasn't been approved by any governments yet.'

'Why not, if it's such a great fuel source?'

'Bureaucracy,' Abby said with a shrug and a sniff.

James looked sideways at her. 'Plus it's about twenty times better at trapping heat in the atmosphere, so global warming will go through the roof if everyone starts using it.'

'It sounds just Lumos's sort of thing,' Beck said harshly. 'It's dangerous, it hurts people, it damages the environment, and it makes a few of their top dogs very rich.' He gave the map a quick scan. *'Probable distribution of MH deposits . . .* Blah, blah . . . Ooh, listen to this. *In order to safeguard the maximization of profits, it is essential that the location of Island Alpha is not revealed as a potential fuel source* . . . Typical Lumos. Don't tell anyone because they might shut it down before we make any money.'

He crumpled the paper up and thrust it at Abby. 'Here, read it yourself if you must.' And he tramped down the beach to stare out at the sea.

Beck looked out at the waves for a long time. Sometimes he felt tears threatening to well up, but he faced into the wind and his eyes stayed dry. And one thought, one word, blew about inside his head, over and over.

Lumos.

How did they do it? How did they get into absolutely everything? And how was it that everything they touched turned bad?

And what was Steven's connection? What was going on?

He didn't know how long it had been, but suddenly James was at his side.

'Uh, Beck? They'd like to talk to you . . .'

The boys made their way back to the adults. Beck went slowly, kicking the sand along the way.

Abby had smoothed out the map on the sand. Down one side of it was a wiggly line that Beck realized was the coast of Florida. Coloured patches showed where Lumos thought there might be deposits of methane hydrate beneath the sea bed. Dark dots were islands.

'Beck, I've been talking to the captain and he's pretty sure that we're here. This dot is our island.'

Her finger was covering the dot in question and Beck had to move it. It was, without question, a dot.

'I'm just using dead reckoning,' Farrell said, 'based on approximately how far off course we could have got at top speed over that length of time . . . but yes, I think that's probably us.'

It might have been useful information if they'd had some way of communicating with the outside world. As it was, it didn't do them a great deal of good. 'OK, so we know where we are. Still miles from anywhere.'

'Not quite.' Abby moved the hand that had been holding the paper to reveal more markings. There was another, smaller dot, and it was labelled ISLAND ALPHA.

'That's the Lumos base no one's meant to know about . . .'

'If we patched up the lifeboat, we could probably get there.'

'No.' Beck shook his head firmly. 'No way. First rule of survival is you stay put until someone comes to get you. Unless . . .' he added, remembering all the times he *hadn't* stayed put. He had crossed mountains, deserts, jungles . . . 'Unless you've got a very good reason not to. Like, it's a matter of life and death to keep moving. But say someone *does* come to look for us, and they find this island. How will they know where we've gone? We'll have blown our chance to be rescued. If we stay here, we've got food and water . . .'

Although, he had to remind himself, that wasn't entirely true. Water was low and would get lower, and it would take time to make any.

But he so totally did *not* want to put himself at the mercy of the open sea – with an island full of Lumos people at the other side.

'I hear what you're saying, Beck,' Farrell said gently, 'and I agree. But look at it the other way. If there's a base on this island, then there are people there. They must be in communication with the mainland. They certainly have food and water. And whatever you say about the company, Beck, the people there will just be ordinary people like you and me. They'll help us.'

Beck nodded. He badly wanted to believe it was true – that the people who worked for Lumos were just decent, everyday guys. That it was only the ones at the very top who were rotten.

But he had met decent, everyday guys before who worked for Lumos – and somehow they got corrupted too. He wouldn't trust anyone there.

On the other hand, they might be better off at Island Alpha. Especially if there *was* a hurricane coming. Better off than here, anyway.

He looked Farrell square in the eyes. 'You're the sailor. Do you think the lifeboat can get us that far? And how long would it take us?'

It wasn't just that the lifeboat needed to float. Beck needed to be able to keep everyone alive for however long it took.

'I think it can keep us afloat for twenty-four hours,' Farrell said simply. 'And I think that's how long it will take us.'

'Can we beat the hurricane?'

If there was any chance at all that the hurricane

would strike first, they were staying put. It would be mighty rough on the island, but they wouldn't stand a chance in a boat on the open sea.

'We can do it. We'll row like we did last night. Two on the oars, one on the rudder, one resting, and we rotate every hour.'

Beck put his hands on his hips and wandered down the beach to study the wrecked boat. It wasn't *badly* wrecked – just that big crack. The paintwork had also suffered in the beating it had taken in the surf. It was even more flaky and peeling. Beck could just make out the shadow of old lettering on the hull, left over from the boat's last paint job. But the paint-work wasn't a problem. He didn't care what it looked like, as long as it floated.

He *really* didn't want to do this. Beck always reckoned up the odds before he moved on from somewhere: would it be better to stay put? Usually it had always been something like: twenty-five per cent better to stay, seventy-five per cent better to go.

This was more like forty-nine per cent better to stay on the island, fifty-one per cent better to head out for Island Alpha. But those extra couple of percentage points were what made the difference.

He went back to the others, his head already full of plans. First they would have to stockpile a heap of coconuts for the journey . . .

'We'll do it,' he said. 'We'll leave tonight.'

CHAPTER 29

Beck solemnly tied the scrap of bandage firmly around James's wrist. The other boy winced slightly. 'Not too tight?'

James forced a smile. 'I can still feel my fingers. Just.'

'You'll get used to it.' Beck picked up a pebble and another length of bandage and turned to Abby. She silently held out her wrist.

The seasickness tablets had been lost when the boat was wrecked. This was an alternative method. Beck had heard of it but never tried it out. It was an acupuncture technique. Putting pressure on the centre of the wrist was meant to stimulate the nerves in the arm and help the brain ignore the contra-dictory messages it was getting from elsewhere.

Now each of them had a bandage tied round their wrist, with a small pebble inside it applying the pressure.

It was the last precaution they could take before leaving.

'Time to go,' Beck said.

The patched-up boat floated between them while waves gushed around their knees and thighs. It was loaded up with their meagre supplies.

'. . . two, three,' said Farrell, 'and *go*.'

With Abby and James on one side, Farrell and Beck on the other, they ran the boat out into the surf. They had practised the move several times already. The moment the boat was floating they clambered in over the sides. It was awkward because the canvas cover was stretched tight over the front end as part of the repair, and so there was less space for them. Limbs tangled and banged together as they climbed in.

Abby took the tiller and kept the boat facing away from the island. Beck and Farrell grabbed the oars and dug the blades into the water. They heaved with all their strength, pulling the boat towards the breaking waves. Getting through them was just the first of the challenges that lay ahead.

The sun was setting almost directly behind the island. Red light shone between the silhouettes of dark trees. They had left Steven's body there, neatly laid out with his hands on his chest and covered with half a foot of wet sand. It was the best they could do, right now. They couldn't bring him with them and there hadn't been time to dig him a grave. Beck hoped they would get help and return to the island before the crabs had done too much damage.

'Here it comes,' said James from the bow. Beck heard the worry in his voice.

Then the boat shuddered and reared up as it hit the breaker. Spray broke over them and splashed cold against Beck's back, but the boat rose up with it and came crashing down the other side. The pile of coconuts rolled about under the cover, thudding hollowly against the sides of the boat.

'The repair?' Farrell snapped.

There was a pause while James crawled under the cover, dodging the rolling coconuts, and peered at their handiwork. 'Seems to be holding.'

Beck kept up the rhythm, one, two, one, two, hauling on his oar in sync with Farrell. The boat reached the next wave and began to rise up. But this time the wave didn't break over them. They were further out and the waves hadn't reached the critical point where they start to topple over. The third wave, a couple of minutes later, was just a smooth up-and-down.

They were through the surf. The island couldn't hold onto them any longer.

Farrell asked for another report on the repair.

'Still holding.'

The captain just grunted as he and Beck kept rowing.

Abby, at the tiller, had Beck's watch in her hand. She turned in her seat to point the hour hand back at the setting sun and took her reading. Then she pushed the tiller over so that the boat turned onto the course they needed for Island Alpha.

They had used the map on Steven's piece of paper and Beck's watch to calculate a course. There are 360 degrees in a circle, and there were sixty minutes marked on the watch face. That meant that each minute on the watch face was six degrees in real life. They had put the watch on the map and worked out that they had to steer a course of eighty degrees – just a little north of due east.

Soon, Beck hoped, they would be out of the island's shelter and into the Gulf Stream – that would help carry them in the right direction.

Beck felt water sloshing about his ankles. He hoped it came from the waves that had broken over the gunwales, not the leak opening up. 'We need baling,' he said.

Immediately James got to work with the tin box, filling it up with water, which he tipped back into the sea.

And so they kept rowing, while the sun went down and the stars came out.

Beck had bandaged wounds and broken limbs in his time – his own and other people's; until that day, he had never bandaged a boat.

He had heard of the technique, and Farrell had seen it done. The canvas cover was folded to twice its thickness and wrapped the entire way around one end of the boat. They tied it securely in place over the crack with the ropes that had hung around the edges of the life raft.

At first it looked like a joke – as if they had bandaged the boat and hoped it would get better. But once they refloated it, Beck saw the difference immediately. The water pressure outside the boat pushed the cover into the hole and plugged the leak.

The biggest problem was the rope holding the repair in place. Beck had nightmare visions of the cover working loose when they were in the middle of the ocean. He had found some stout, straight sticks and looped the rope around them. By twisting the sticks, he could tighten the rope so that it held. But they would need constant checking and rewinding. Whoever was taking a resting turn, as opposed to rowing or steering, would also have to check the rope and bale out any water that made it through the canvas.

No one was going to get much sleep. But, Beck told himself, it was only twenty-four hours – that was what the captain had said. No one can keep going for ever, but once you're in a routine it's very easy to just put your mind into neutral and slog on. Then you can collapse when you reach your destination.

No one spoke much. There were single words, like: 'Time?' or 'Course?' That was all. Talk just made you thirsty, and no one felt like making conversation. The further they got from the island, the more they knew they were at the mercy of the repair. If the boat chose to sink, there would come a point when they were just too far away to swim back.

For the first hour Abby was in charge of steering, but Beck still kept his own eyes on the stars. He was pleased to see that she maintained the course well. He had to remind himself that she might be a completely different creature to him, with a different world view and different values – but she wasn't stupid. Far from it.

Once the sun had gone down, they were back to navigating by the North Star. It was the only star that was fixed. All the others moved, eventually. You couldn't see it happening unless you paid very close attention, but over the course of the night the entire starscape above them would slowly spin round. You couldn't just pick a star and say 'Aim the boat at that one.' The boat would end up going in a huge curve around the ocean as it followed the moving star. The only thing you could do was make sure that the North Star was always above a particular mark on the side of the boat. Even that wouldn't work over large distances, but the journey to Island Alpha wasn't that long – not compared to the size of the planet. In an aeroplane it would have been a few minutes' flight. But in their little boat, crawling across the face of a great sea, it would take at least twenty-four hours.

After an hour, everyone changed position. Beck had been at the left-hand oar, so it was his turn to rest in the bow. James took the right oar, Farrell took the tiller, Abby moved up to the left oar.

To get to the bow, Beck had to duck under the canvas cover. He studied his handiwork carefully, though it was too dark to see much. The canvas seemed to be doing its job. He baled for a few minutes, then tried to get some sleep for the rest of his allotted hour.

It seemed like only seconds before the next shift and he was back on an oar again. Then it was an hour on the tiller, fighting to keep his eyes open and make sure that the North Star was in the right position. Then back on an oar, then back to an hour of blissful rest in the bow . . .

The chime from Beck's watch announced another change of shift. He and Farrell paused in their rowing and stretched. Beck winced as he felt his joints crack, and blood rushed into muscles that had become tired and cramped. It was the end of his third shift on the left-hand oar. That made it eight o'clock in the morning. They had been at sea for over twelve hours.

They were rowing east, so he'd had his back to the sunrise and hadn't been able to see it easily. He had watched as grey light spread across the ocean and colour returned to the world. The sea slowly turned blue. Abby, at the tiller, slowly materialized as a person rather than just a shape. She was fiddling with the bandage on her wrist. She looked tired and strained.

'I'll get James. You set your watch,' Farrell said. He turned in his seat and stretched out a leg to prod the other boy. James was fast asleep in the bow, his head resting on a lifejacket.

They were back to navigating by the sun again. They had agreed on how to do this the previous night. Unlike the North Star, the sun *did* move. So, every quarter of an hour, Beck wanted whoever was at the tiller to take a fresh bearing and keep them on course. With all the ocean to go wrong in, even a little error could result in them missing their destination by many miles.

He was just setting the alarm for fifteen minutes when something bumped into the boat. It didn't feel like much, just a light *thud*. Beck assumed the bow had just slapped against a wave at a slightly sharper angle than usual.

But then it happened again, and this time Beck felt the shudder through the boat.

A third thud made him clutch at the side to balance himself. 'Hey, what . . . ?'

James gave a low moan. His mouth hung open and his eyes were wide. Slowly he lifted an arm and pointed. Beck followed the direction of his finger, out to sea.

A triangular, dark grey fin broke the surface of the water a few metres away. Beneath it there was just the suggestion of a dark, sleek body before the whole thing disappeared underwater with barely a ripple.

'It's a sh—' James breathed. His chest began to heave up and down as he fought back panic. 'It's a sh— It's a *shark*!'

CHAPTER 30

Beck's mind raced. He had seen what sharks could do.

That time on the raft, off the coast of Colombia, with Chrissy and Marco: just a tiny trail of blood from a spilled can of fish guts had provoked an attack from a tiger shark. A shark at one end of an Olympic-sized swimming pool could smell a single drop of blood at the other. And they moved like torpedoes, accelerating up to forty miles per hour quicker than a car.

But what was attracting this one? No one was bleeding . . .

The boat shook with another thud. This shark was definitely attacking.

'For some reason we've upset it,' Beck said.

They could work out why later. 'It's OK,' he added quickly, to stop James from freaking out altogether. 'It just needs to know we are in charge. If a shark attacks you when you're swimming, and you don't have a knife or a speargun, then you hit it where it's sensitive – like its nose, or its eyes or gills.'

'OK.' Farrell took command. 'James, Abby, grab your oars. When it comes close, *whack it*.'

They didn't need to be told twice, scrambling to their feet and pulling the oars out of the rowlocks. They stood poised, oars at the ready, one on either side of the boat, and waited for the shark to make its next move.

Beck ran through his memories to think of anything they could have done to make the shark think they were edible. What else made sharks attack boats?

Sharks were attracted by electrical fields, and by irregular vibrations. The wrong sort of vibration through the water could make a shark think it was attacking a weak, struggling animal.

He remembered video footage from early 2013 of a great white shark that had attacked a fishing boat off Australia. But that boat had had an engine – a small outboard motor. The experts thought it might have been the electrical impulses that had attracted it. Plus, the fishermen on the boat had been idiots, deliberately trying to wind the shark up.

He still couldn't think of a reason why the shark should attack this boat.

Bright colours could do it – their tiny brains mistook them for fish scales. Maybe the boat's white paint was attracting it?

'There!' Abby interrupted Beck's thoughts. The shark's fin broke the surface right next to them. She tried to lift the oar, and overbalanced. Farrell caught her before she fell over, and then lunged to catch the oar before it disappeared over the side.

'Mum!'

'It's surprisingly heavy,' Abby told her son through gritted teeth.

'If you can't lift the oar, just poke it – hard,' Beck suggested. 'Rest it on the side of the boat and use it like a giant billiard cue.'

He ran his brief glimpse of the shark through his memory. Its fin and back were a slick dark grey.

Great whites, the world's largest predator sharks, were that colour. But they were also quite bulky, while this one was slim and streamlined. A great white's fin was tall and ragged; this one's was smooth. No, Beck was pretty certain it was another tiger shark, like his old friend from Colombia.

The first fact that came to mind, for both sorts of shark, was that they didn't usually attack humans. He scanned the sea for any further sign of the big fish. How much damage could it do? The boat was reasonably sturdy – he doubted the creature could bite a hole in it. And, on its own, it probably couldn't overturn the boat. But if it got two or three friends in, then it might be another matter. Beck had seen the ocean churned up by a school of sharks in a feeding frenzy: a storm of razor-sharp teeth, and jaws that could bite through boats.

No – the humans in the boat needed to persuade the shark to be somewhere else, right now.

'There!' Farrell called.

It had returned. Unfortunately it was now coming straight towards the bow. James and Abby were in the middle of the boat and they couldn't swing the oars round to hit it. Then the fin vanished as the shark dived. There was another shudder, and this time a ripping sound too. The canvas cover shifted and a gush of water squirted through the crack.

'It's attacking the cover!' Beck shouted. *That* was what was doing it. Something like a loose end of canvas must have been flapping about underwater. The shark maybe thought it was a dying fish. Then, every time it tried to snatch the fish in its jaws, it bumped into something solid and heavy. So the shark was getting angrier and angrier, and it was taking it out on the boat.

Another rip, and the canvas came away completely. It vanished over the side before Beck could lunge to catch it. Water surged up through the crack. Within seconds it was washing around his feet.

The shark thrashed around in the water a few metres away. The cover must have got caught in its teeth and the shark was trying to get rid of it. Beck only processed this with part of his mind. He was concentrating on baling for his life, using the tin box to throw the water out as soon as it came in.

It was a losing battle. The water just came in too fast.

And now the shark had got rid of the cover and its fin was heading back towards the boat.

James balanced his oar on the gunwale, aimed carefully, and thrust. 'Got it!' he shouted with glee. 'Right on the nose!'

The shark turned away and vanished underwater. James had given it a good thwack. What with that, and the unexpected taste of the canvas, it had suddenly lost interest in the strange big white fish-that-wasn't-a-fish.

It was a temporary triumph.

'We're abandoning ship. Everyone, lifejackets on,' Farrell ordered. 'You too, Beck.'

'But . . .' Beck protested, though he knew the captain was right. The boat was a goner. He just hated to give up. He hated being forced to swim in a shark-infested sea even more.

There were a few moments of fumbling with lifejackets and their straps. Beck felt for the mouthpiece on the end of the dangling tube and began to blow. With each breath he felt the lifejacket swelling around his body until the sleek plastic was rigid, like shiny, yellow body armour.

It wasn't really abandoning ship. It was more like the ship abandoning them. It went down bow first. The sea came in and took them. Beck kept his eyes peeled for fins.

Abby and James both stared at the water advancing up their bodies, as if a shark might leap out at any moment from between their knees and attack them. Farrell's face was unreadable.

'James, grab the water!' Beck snapped. The silver water bag was floating past and James quickly took hold of it. Farrell grasped the first-aid box. Beck took one last look around for something – anything – that might come in useful. If you hadn't planned for a disaster and disaster struck anyway, then you took what you could. You worked out what to do with it later.

He wished he'd known disaster was coming earlier so he could have taken some things from the ship – but wishing gets you nowhere, so he stopped wasting the brainpower on it.

A length of bandage from the first-aid kit curled

and twisted in the water. He grabbed hold of it and wrapped it securely around one arm.

The water had felt comfortably warm when they were in the surf back on the island. Now the cold chill quickly ate into Beck's body – legs, thighs, waist, chest. Then he felt the lifejacket take over. The straps were taking his weight. He was no longer standing on the boat, he was floating in the ocean with his head only centimetres above the sea.

The bow tilted further and further down until the boat was hanging vertical in the water and just the stern bobbed above the waves. And then it stopped sinking. There was an airtight barrel tied beneath the helmsman's bench that gave it buoyancy. The boat would never completely sink while it was there.

But that was the only good news.

They were a hundred miles from anywhere. They had no boat. They had no way of reaching Island Alpha, or the mainland, and somewhere nearby there was a hungry shark.

CHAPTER 31

Beck fought back the panic.

He had never been in such dire straits as this ever before.

Yes, he had been stranded, and in tight spots – many of them – but he had always been on land, able to get his hands on something that would keep him alive. Food, even if it was only insects. Water, even if it was his own wee. And there had always been the hope of rescue, or of being able to make his way to a safe place.

Here, he had nothing – just a half-submerged, upturned raft and a sea full of hungry sharks.

He knew he was in trouble.

Miles from land. No kind of shelter. The sun would get higher and broil them alive, if the sharks didn't take them first. He squeezed his eyes tight shut in despair. *It was over.*

But then it came like a whisper into his head.

Never say die, Beck . . .

Two human figures moved for a moment among the dancing patterns at the back of his closed eyes. He knew immediately who they were.

He was a small boy, crying because he had fallen and hurt his knee. *Never say die.* He had been trudging across Dartmoor, frozen and soaked to the bone, just wanting to give up and go to sleep. *Never say die.* It had been the motto of their lives.

Beck opened his eyes and the figures vanished. Their memory remained. 'I won't die, Mum . . . I won't die, Dad,' he murmured.

It had all taken only a couple of seconds.

'OK,' he said out loud. He marshalled his thoughts. Priorities: stay out of the water as much as possible. Defend against sharks. Conserve food and water.

The first was relatively easy. 'We need to take turns up on the boat. An hour each. Um –

alphabetical order? I suppose that makes you first,' he said to Abby.

'And you second, and me last!' James protested.

Beck glared at him. 'Fine,' he said sarcastically. 'How about age order? Then I'll be last!'

'That's enough!' Farrell took command. 'We'll go clockwise in the order we're in now, which means James, Beck, Abby, then me. James, let's give you a hand . . .'

James didn't need to be told twice. With much splashing and kicking and shoving from below, he wriggled onto the narrow platform that was the boat's floating stern.

He was about two centimetres out of the water, and balanced precariously. Beck reckoned he wouldn't have much chance if a shark decided to give the boat a knock. But being out of the water meant being out of the cold. The rest of them clung onto the lifelines down the side of the boat.

'Here, take these.' Farrell passed the boxes and the water up to James.

'Hey,' James said, 'we can still make water, like we did on the island!' He looked so pleased with himself that Beck managed a discreet smile. Someone else with the never-say-die attitude.

'And this . . .' One of the boat's oars was floating nearby: Beck pulled it in and passed it up to James. 'Whoever's on the boat will need to be our main shark lookout – and shark defender. See anything?'

James quickly scanned their limited horizon, turning in a full circle. 'No fins. Not at the moment.'

'OK, what next?' Abby asked.

Beck thought for a moment, then started to unwrap the length of bandage from around his arm. 'Sharks don't like large groups – they prefer to pick off individuals. So we all stay together. I'm going to make sure of that . . .'

It took a few minutes, but he was able to thread the bandage through the straps of each person's lifejacket.

'This way,' he said as he tied the last knot to the captain's lifejacket, 'we can rest and no one will drift away.'

'And the sharks?' Abby reminded him.

'Right. We only move about when we have to. And we do it slowly. Make as few splashes as possible. Especially avoid lots of kicking.' He said this with a sideways glance at James, who had been churning the water up with his feet as he wriggled up onto the boat. 'Try not make the sharks think we're an injured animal.'

Beck thought again. His experience with sharks hadn't been all bad. He had scuba-dived with them in the Red Sea. When they weren't trying to eat you, they were amazing creatures – lithe and graceful, flicking through the water like lazy torpedoes with the tiniest motions of their fins. As long as the sharks were not hungry, and not disturbed, they were safe.

They'd had a guide armed with a spear gun, but that was just precautionary. His job was to keep an eye on the sharks and spot the ones likely to turn nasty. He had told Beck what to look out for – and Beck now passed the information on to the others.

'Just because you can see a fin doesn't mean it's going to attack. If they're just swimming about, smooth and slow, that means they're passing through. Maybe they're curious. If they start swimming quickly, dodging this way and that – that means they're getting agitated. And if they arch their back, put their head up, start zigzagging towards you – that means they're attacking. When they do that, whoever's up on the boat gets ready to hit out again. Right, James?'

James was pale, but he clutched the oar in both hands and braced himself. 'Right. Thanks.'

'Cool. Next . . .' Beck looked at Abby and couldn't help grinning. 'Do you want the good news or the bad?'

Her eyes narrowed; she was obviously wondering what he could possibly find amusing at a time like this. 'Let's have the good.'

'Sharks see in black and white to give them a clear contrast between shapes. There's a particularly poisonous sea snake that colours itself black and white to warn the sharks off. Which means that a lot of other creatures are black and white too, to fool it. So, with that black-and-white outfit you're wearing, hopefully the sharks will think you're a poisonous snake and won't come near.'

James actually laughed for a moment, and even Farrell bit back a smile. Abby's face went cold.

'How reassuring. And the bad news?'

'You need to take your ring off. And I'm removing my watch too.' He unclasped it from around his wrist. 'Anything like jewellery gives off glints and reflections, which they mistake for fish scales.'

He put his hands underwater and felt for the pocket where he had put James's silver ring earlier. He tugged the zip open and slid his watch in to join it.

Abby held up her hand and studied the ring. She looked very doubtful. 'I don't know, Beck. It's very valuable. I wouldn't want it to fall out of a pocket.'

'Mum!' James protested. 'Just do it! Unless you want to hold your hand out of the water for ever?'

She scowled at him.

'I've got a pocket with a zip,' Beck assured her. 'I can look after it.'

To his amazement, Abby still looked uncertain. Eventually she reached a decision and pulled the ring off her finger.

'That won't be necessary.' She slid her ring into one of her lifejacket pockets and zipped it up. 'Happy?'

Beck didn't bother answering. He still couldn't

believe that anyone would think twice about taking off a silver ring if it meant they had a better chance of staying alive. But that was her problem.

'OK,' he said. 'Now, the sun's going to be harsh. Whoever's up on the boat, you can take off your life-jacket and wear it like a hat. The rest of us will have to shelter in that person's shadow as much as we can. Captain, we'll need your shirt – we're going to set up the still again. We'll put it on the boat with James.'

Farrell rolled his eyes in a good-humoured way, and nodded.

'And . . .' This was the key question that Beck carefully hadn't been asking out loud. But they all deserved to know the answer. 'Will they still be looking for us?'

'Yes,' Farrell said. 'When the rescue services don't find us along the route we should have taken, they'll broaden the search. They'll find us – if we are lucky. It's just a matter of how many boats and planes they use. The more they use, the sooner they'll manage it.'

He sounded hopeful, but Beck noticed him bite

his lip for a moment when he had finished speaking. Was Farrell as sure as he sounded? Or, like a good captain, was he just trying to keep morale up?

Beck let it pass, because the last thing anyone needed was him pointing out, *You don't really mean that, do you?*

'Cool,' he said instead. 'OK, I've still got that flare.' He patted his pocket to confirm it, and felt the thin metal tube there. 'Have you still got yours?' he asked Abby. She nodded. 'Then we keep a lookout, and if necessary we'll fire the flare off. But we only do it if they're close enough to notice us.'

Beck had had another reason for asking about rescue. It was the sharks, again. Sharks were more likely to attack at night.

He didn't tell anyone this. There was no point in making them worry. They had the whole day ahead of them. He would let them know about night attacks if they were still there when the sun went down.

CHAPTER 32

Time passed, very slowly. The small party huddled in James's shadow, moving and talking as little as possible. There wasn't much to say, and they had to conserve energy.

Eventually James's hour was up and it was Beck's turn to go on the boat. The sun was well up by now. The small platform of the stern was dry and warm to the touch. James actually looked quite relieved to be slipping back into the water, where it was cooler.

Beck gloomily surveyed what he could see from his vantage point. Just more sea. No signs of fins – good. No ships either – bad. He glanced up.

The trail of an airliner was making its way across the sky, marking out a line of pure white behind it. He gave a wry smile. It had been just like this twenty-four hours ago, their first new day after the ship sank. If only just one airliner would fly lower – like, three miles lower – then they might have a chance of being spotted . . .

His fingers were picking idly at the flaky paint of the lifeboat. It passed the time, if nothing else. Without realizing it, he had exposed most of a letter 'O'.

After a while he glanced up again, and this time his eyes narrowed. The trail was still there. Usually they turned fluffy within minutes; less than an hour and they were gone, or just a very faint smear of white cloud. This one was still sharply defined.

It stayed that way for most of Beck's allotted time on the boat. Every now and again he looked up at it to check. This meant one thing. It was a clear sign of low pressure – which indicated that a storm was on its way. Was it the hurricane he had spotted on the weather radar? Or just – *just!* – a normal storm?

Either way it would be very bad news for their small party of survivors. But it would help keep the sharks away . . .

Maybe.

He deliberately looked down, pushing the telltale cloud away from his mind. Again, there was nothing he could do about it. If the storm struck, it struck. They would have to ride it out as best they could.

Beck's fingers were still working away at the paint. After the 'O' there was what looked like the first part of an 'S'. Before it, he found half an 'M'.

Suddenly Beck's eyes went wide and he stared down at the letters. No! It couldn't be!

But he couldn't let it rest. He picked away – harder now, digging his fingernails into the paint to tear it away.

And then there was no doubt about it. Beneath the paint were the letters L.U.M.O.S.

'Lumos . . .' he breathed.

Abby looked up sharply. 'What about it?'

Beck paused, then sighed. 'Nothing. This boat belonged to Lumos. That's all.'

He shouldn't have been surprised. Steven had been working for the organization, and Steven had been the one to get him on the ship. So it shouldn't be a shock to find that the ship also belonged to Lumos.

Beck cocked his head and looked thoughtfully at the letters. It was the first time he had seen them picked out like that, with full stops in between. It meant that Lumos wasn't just a name; it stood for something. He hadn't realized. He wondered what it was.

'Losers Unite . . .' he murmured, but he couldn't think of what the last three letters might stand for.

And then a shock like freezing water seemed to flow over him.

'Beck . . . ?' Farrell sounded worried.

Beck must have gasped out loud. His mind had offered up another connection. How had he seen that? Maybe it was because the first three letters he had cleared away were the 'M.O.S.'

Beck scrabbled at his zipped-up pocket and pulled out James's ring. He angled it so that he could read the words engraved on the inside.

MASTERY. OBEDIENCE. SUCCESS. LOGIC. UNDERSTANDING.

That was how he had read them when he first saw them. But they were engraved in a circle. Any of

them could be the first words. Say you started with
LOGIC . . .

LOGIC. UNDERSTANDING. MASTERY. OBEDIENCE.
SUCCESS.

L.U.M.O.S.

His mouth dropped open. He stared at James.
James met his eyes briefly, and then his face went
pale and he looked away.

'You . . . you said your grandfather founded the
family business . . .' Beck stammered. 'The family
business . . . is *Lumos*?'

'Yes!' James blurted. 'Lumos. It's all about
Lumos. No, wrong. It's all about you, Beck Granger.
Everything that has happened has been about *you*.'

CHAPTER 33

James fell silent, though his chest was heaving and tears brimmed in his eyes.

Abby gazed at him with tenderness. 'James, sweetheart, you knew this moment would come. Don't let Mummy down now.'

'Let you down?' James gasped. 'Mum, *you* got us into this, and *he's* doing his best to get us out of it! Can't you see that?'

She just rolled her eyes and looked away, like a mother with a toddler having a tantrum.

'Abby, just what the— Just what is going on?' Farrell demanded.

'Are you going to tell him?' James asked Abby.

'I don't see that it makes much difference,' she said quietly. Then, more conversationally, 'Yes,

Beck, Lumos is the family business. It was founded by my father, Edwin Blake. I've worked for him ever since I was a child – he taught me everything he knew – and lately I've been training James up to work alongside me, to take over one day. This journey was part of his apprenticeship. I'm the "cleaner".'

'A . . . cleaner?' Beck repeated. He couldn't quite picture Abby in an apron, pushing the cleaning trolley around the offices.

'She cleans up the company's problems,' James muttered.

'What kind of problems?'

'Problems,' said Abby brightly, and then her voice changed, and darkness passed across her face. 'Problems like Beck Granger, the most annoying, obstructive, interfering brat who has ever walked upon the Earth. Problems that will insist on sticking their nose into our business, over and over and over again. Or problems like Beck Granger's parents, who started it. We thought the problems would go away when they did – and, of course, that's what happened, for a few years.' She paused.

'Until Beck got older. Then the problems started up again. Whenever we have a money-losing set-back, Daddy makes a note of who to blame. He will allow anyone to hurt us once. Accidents do happen, after all. No one's perfect. But if the same name starts showing up over and over again ... You, Beck, have cost us an oil refinery and a uranium mine, and several people with useful skills that we liked to employ from time to time have ended up behind bars. You have become a problem. Do you get my meaning?'

Beck couldn't speak.

Deep down inside he felt energy begin to flow, ready to surge and explode out of him, and do ... what? Throw himself at her? Hold her underwater until she drowned?

Ever since he had learned that his parents had been murdered, he'd had dreams about this moment. Tracking down and confronting the killers. Reducing them to quivering, helpless heaps. Closing off every escape route, every option so that they had no choice but to face him, and then he would destroy them. Somehow.

In practice what he'd do, he knew, is hand them over to the law. Vengeance makes for good movies, but it's rubbish in practice. Killing his parents' killers would just reduce him to their level. Much better to get them behind bars for the rest of their lives, where every day until they died they would know that they had failed and that he was still alive and well.

He had fantasized about it happening in many different ways, but he hadn't expected it to be like this.

'But,' he added, 'if all this was about getting rid of me, it's a pretty stupidly complicated way of doing it. I mean, I go to school every day. You could have killed me with a faked hit-and-run accident. Or you could have . . . you could have just burned down the house! How did organizing a cruise come into it?'

Abby shook her head. 'It had to be this way,' she said decisively. 'It had to be on one of your adventures. You had to be seen to fail, and we had to discourage all the little Beck Granger wannabes out there.'

Unlike Beck, Farrell was decidedly uncalm. 'You

can't mean that!' he exploded. 'Beck . . . Beck's a *boy*!'

Abby regarded him coolly. 'And just think what harm he could do once he's a man. We had the PR all set up – a carefully planned set of press releases that we would publish over the next few months, after his tragic death, to show how the mighty Beck Granger was just a spoiled brat who used his celebrity status to insist on taking the *Sea Cloud* even though we told him it wasn't safe, and how he bullied a sad, weak wreck of a ship's captain into pressing on . . .'

Farrell's face showed that he was slowly working out what Beck had realized immediately he learned the truth about Abby's work. Somehow, *she* had been responsible for the sabotage of the *Sea Cloud*. And the captain had none of Beck's reservations about taking revenge. He let go of the boat with one hand, then the other; he turned towards her and said, almost conversationally, 'I am going to take your neck, lady, and—'

'And nothing,' James said sharply. It was a bark of command. He might have been full of doubts, but there was one thing he knew: no one was going to attack his mother. 'There's two of us, Captain, and you might be bigger than both of us, but we have . . .' He seemed to be casting around for the right word.

' "Skills" is the word James is looking for,' Abby said. Her light-hearted, casual tone had turned into something as cold as ice and hard as steel. 'Self-defence skills. Without going into details, let's just say that men do not attack me and live to tell the tale.'

Slowly, very slowly, Farrell subsided.

'Now, where was I? Oh yes, the plan.' Abby's bright, chatty side made an abrupt reappearance. 'By the time we were through with your memory, Beck, you wouldn't have been a tragic loss. More like "good riddance". Everyone would say you had it coming. And we would have tarred your dear Uncle Al with the same brush . . . make sure people were asking why he had allowed a fourteen-year-old to get into such dangerous situations . . . And so on. He would have been destroyed too. In short, a clear win all round.'

Beck started to laugh. He couldn't help himself. Fear. Anger. Nerves. Shock.

Now it was Abby's turn to stare.

'What is so funny?'

'Lumos!' Beck's shoulders shook. 'Lumos strikes again. You just can't do it properly. I don't know what the plan was, but I bet it didn't involve you ending up shipwrecked along with the rest of us. You want to know how I can keep interfering with your sick little plans? It's because they're always so rubbish! You say I cost you a uranium mine? No, you cost that *yourselves*! First, you didn't spend enough money in the first place to keep the containment tanks secure. Then you hired a couple of amateurs to try and kill me. You'll spend a pound to save a penny, won't you? You *could* spend a bit more and keep everyone happy, including yourselves. You could get rich *and* use all your technology to help people . . . But no. No, no, no. You wouldn't be rich *enough*. So you spend as little as you can, and it goes wrong.'

'Shut up, you little brat. You know nothing about business.'

'Go on.' Beck waved his hand airily. He met her hostile glare with the broadest, friendliest smile he could produce. 'Go on. Tell me what was supposed to happen and what went wrong.'

CHAPTER 34

Abby kept glaring.

Beck's opinion of Lumos couldn't sink any lower, after all, and the fact was, the plan *had* gone wrong. He was better than his enemies, in so many ways.

'I'll tell it all, Beck, because it doesn't matter. You are about to die anyway.' She stared at him.

'I hired Steven Holbrook – he knew nothing, of course – and I used his connection with your uncle to get you onto this trip,' said Abby. 'Yes, the ship was an old Lumos vessel – it used to be the executive yacht for the management team, many years ago.'

So, Beck thought, that explained its ramshackle appearance. An old ship, done up with the minimum outlay – typical Lumos.

'And all the crew were your people?'

'Not all,' Farrell snapped. He hadn't stopped glaring at Abby. If human eyes were lasers, then Abby's head would have exploded a long time ago.

'No, not all,' she agreed. 'We needed a proper captain, of course, so we hired a down-and-out old sailor – he was unemployable because he managed to lose his last ship in a typhoon by ignoring the weather reports. So obviously, when I offered him a job, he jumped at the chance without enquiring into it too closely.'

Farrell's eyes narrowed to tiny slits of hate and anger. He ground out his words through clenched teeth. 'And, of course, having already lost one ship through carelessness, the fact that I was in command of this ship would just add credibility to the story when it hit the press?'

'Well, naturally. And I came along because – well, believe it or not, Beck, you were right about our hiring amateurs. That is one of the key reasons our Australian venture failed. I've always known that if you want a job done properly, then it is best done yourself. I was going to oversee this personally.

When we were all up on the bridge, I put a virus into the ship's systems—'

'How?' Farrell demanded.

'It's—' James began, but his mother interrupted.

'Oh, come, Captain, let a girl keep some secrets.'

'Why didn't you abandon ship at the same time as the crew?' Beck asked. 'Why were you still there when the bomb went off?'

Abby paused and pulled a face. Beck wondered if this was the point where the plan had gone wrong.

'We would have set it off by remote control once we were in the boat and clear of the ship. Except for Steven. Ah, dear Steven. The man had no idea, no idea at all. He confronted us. He had worked out that something was up. He was snooping around and worked out that there weren't really any luxury facilities behind all those locked doors on the ship. I expect he was going to bring it up in the morning, except that he bumped into us on our way to the boat and overheard . . . Well, never mind what he overheard, but he learned he was in way over his head. But he still confronted us. There was . . . let's say, a scuffle, in which James and I were forced to use the skills he was careful to mention just now. But not before Steven tried to grab the remote control – and that was when the bomb went off.'

'And so we all abandoned ship, and it sank,' Farrell said. He still hadn't quite unclamped his jaw. 'And your friends never came back for you.'

Abby looked distinctly annoyed. 'Because Steven distracted me, I forgot my bag. My phone was in it.' Beck remembered that too – her sudden insistence that she had to go back for it, just as the ship was going down. 'They had no way of tracking us. And so we were lumbered with you.'

'And suddenly it became important to keep me alive,' Beck said dryly.

'Well, you *are* the expert.' She gave him a forced fake smile.

Farrell exploded in rage. 'You sick, twisted, low-life . . .' He trailed off, running out of words. Then he rallied. '*Murderous* . . .' Another lapse into silence. Abby kept her face impassive. 'We were going to drown like rats just so you could . . . could . . . And Steven? You killed him too, didn't you?'

'Obviously. And planted enough information on

him to ensure that we would launch off towards Island Alpha. Fortunately I had that memo on me. I had no intention of sitting rotting on that tiny rock we found ourselves on.'

Beck threw his hands in the air. 'And so – typical Lumos – it still goes wrong, and here we are.'

'Speak for yourself,' Abby said. '*I'm* about to be rescued.'

Her hand came out of the water, holding the flare that had been in her pocket. Beck prepared to throw himself aside, because for one moment he thought she actually intended to shoot him with it. But she aimed it above her head and pulled on the tab. There was a bang like a gunshot, and the flare soared up into the air. High above their heads it burst into white flame.

CHAPTER 35

'What—?' Beck began. And then he realized that he could hear rotor blades. In fact, he had been hearing them for some time. He had just been so distracted by Abby's story that he hadn't registered the helicopter that she had obviously spotted on the horizon. *Some survivor you are!* he snapped at himself.

'Lumos will have been looking for me ever since I failed to check in yesterday. I'm far too valuable an asset for them to let me perish so easily,' Abby said calmly. 'And James, of course,' she added as an afterthought.

The helicopter was only a small dot on the horizon, but it soon grew larger. All eyes stayed on it, and no one spoke as it roared towards them. It circled around while the crew had a good look down at them. It was a big model, something like a Sea King, painted bright yellow.

Squinting up against the sun, Beck could just see the word LUMOS painted on its belly.

His heart sank. For a moment he'd hoped that it was from one of the search-and-rescue organizations. No such luck.

It slowed and hovered ten metres above them, like a giant metal dragonfly. The roar of its engine made any speech impossible. The downdraught from its rotors flattened the sea around them. Then the figure of a man appeared from its side, dangling from a winch. He looked like a slimmed-down spaceman, in helmet and drysuit. He was lowered towards them, spinning around slowly until his legs reached the water. He gestured towards James.

James gave Beck and Farrell a final glance. His face was like a death mask. Every human emotion had been pushed down deep inside where it needn't bother him again.

'Thanks for saving my life,' he said simply.

'Don't keep the man waiting, sweetheart,' Abby chided.

He ignored her. 'It's the ring . . .' James spoke clearly. Beck looked at him blankly. 'She used the ring to sabotage the ship.' Abby stared at her son, but he met her glare. 'Oh, come on, Mum, what does it matter? The ring's a Bluetooth microcomputer. That's how she transferred the virus. Just so you know.'

And then he pushed himself away from the boat and quickly splashed his way towards the man, who helped him get his arms and shoulders through a large loop that hung from the bottom of the line.

Farrell and Beck exchanged glances. Beck felt the frustration tear at him – just having to sit there while the others were rescued. But what could they do? They were in no position to take over a helicopter.

'Sir!' Farrell shouted. It was a forlorn hope, Beck thought, but it was worth trying. 'You have to help us! This woman is a criminal! You can't just leave us here!'

The man merely glanced over at him, then looked up at the hovering machine and jerked a thumb up. He and James rose smoothly out of the water. James was pulled into the cabin, and seconds later the man was back. Now Abby swam over to him.

'Give my regards to the sharks!' she called. There was a huge smile on her face as she was lifted up.

Sick at heart, Beck watched her disappear into the cabin. All the fears and worries he had felt when the boat sank beneath them came flooding back. *Never say die?* Who was he kidding? They had squeezed a few more hours of life out of the ocean, that was all.

He and Farrell could make their water last a bit longer, now that there were only two of them. But they had the rest of the day ahead, and then, at night time, the sharks would come.

A storm was on its way, which would churn up the sea and send thousands of tons of water crashing down on them. They would drown . . . if the sharks hadn't eaten them first. And the worst of it was, the helicopter would no doubt report that it had rescued all the survivors from the *Sea Cloud*. The search would be called off. No one would come for them.

Sudden tears pricked his eyes – not just for himself, but for James. What chance had that boy ever had? Following his mother around the world and holding her bags while she killed people . . . How could he ever have hoped to learn right from wrong?

'Beck? Beck!' Farrell had to call his name a couple of times to get his attention. It dawned on Beck that the helicopter hadn't moved. It was still hovering over them. He looked up with a sudden surge of hope.

The man was coming down towards them again.

CHAPTER 36

'This is not acceptable!'

The first thing Beck heard as he was hauled into the cabin was Abby's voice: she was raging at the man in charge of the winch.

The cabin was bare and functional. James had taken one of the few seats. He and Abby had silver thermal blankets draped over their shoulders. James had pulled his tight around himself and was staring at the floor. He very carefully didn't meet Beck's eye. Through the cockpit door, Beck could see the back of the pilot's head as he sat at the controls. He was peering out of the window as he kept the helicopter hovering in the same position.

The winch man was unapologetic. 'Orders of your father, ma'am. *All* survivors were to be rescued.'

'But—'

'He said he will be attending to them personally, ma'am, once he arrives on Island Alpha. Over there.'

These last words were aimed at Beck, and accompanied by a shove in his back. The man pushed him towards the rear of the cabin. It was a large space, for carrying cargo rather than people. Beck hunkered down on the metal floor, hugging his knees, and watched as the man pressed buttons to lower his colleague to retrieve Captain Farrell.

'Attending to them personally?' Abby scowled, hands on hips, and for just a moment Beck wondered if he'd caught a glimpse of fear. Was her father the kind of guy who went easy on people who failed in their tasks? He was prepared to bet he wasn't – even when it was his own daughter. Maybe Abby was in for more than just a ticking-off.

But if there was fear, it was only a flash. Abby threw a cold smile at Beck. 'Very well,' she said.

He shivered, and it wasn't because he didn't have a thermal blanket. Whatever she was in for, he was in for worse.

Farrell was pulled aboard and the winch man slid

the door shut. He shouted something into a micro-phone, and the pilot nodded back at him in acknowledgement. The floor tilted and the helicopter started to move again. Beck felt his ears pop as they rose higher and the engine noise settled down to a loud, steady drone.

Farrell had squatted down next to Beck.

Beck put his mouth close to the captain's ear. 'Her father wants to attend to us personally.'

His mouth tightened into a grim line. 'Not if I can strangle him first!'

The flight took nearly an hour. There was nothing to do except sit there. Abby spent much of the time speaking on a phone produced by one of the crew, or sitting talking to James. Or maybe she was talk-ing at him. She looked excited, her gestures emphatic. James just sat and stared at the floor, sometimes muttering a one-word response.

It was a rough ride: the massive engine above them made the whole frame shake. Sitting on the metal floor meant that the vibrations travelled up Beck's spine. It was far from comfortable. Even so, he couldn't help noticing that as they flew on, the ride grew even rougher. At first the cabin just rocked a little; he put it down to air currents – it was only every few minutes. But then it began to happen more frequently, and the rocking grew stronger.

Finally Abby stood up and made her way to the rear of the cabin. Suddenly the helicopter gave a great lurch, and she clutched at the ceiling for support.

'Five minutes to Island Alpha,' she said. The helicopter shuddered again, almost as if it had hit something. 'Should be there just in time for the hurricane,' she added.

Beck and Farrell exchanged glances. What with the other things on his mind, Beck had actually forgotten about it. Abby actually sounded as if she was looking forward to it.

The helicopter tilted, but this time it was circling, coming in to land.

Abby pointed out of the side window. 'And there it is. Take a good look.'

Beck glanced casually out of the window, not that interested in an island he might never be leaving. Then he looked again, surprised.

Island Alpha wasn't an island. It was a giant drilling rig. Four giant metal pillars rose up out of the water like small skyscrapers. At the top was an impossible collection of girders and platforms and cabins, clinging together in a way that seemed to defy gravity. The helicopter landing platform jutted out from the side, fifty metres above the water – a large metal slab marked with the letter 'H'.

The paper that Abby had planted on Steven had talked about experimental drilling for methane hydrate. This must be where Lumos was doing its work.

'Wait!' Beck protested. 'We're going to be on a rig in a hurricane? That's suicide!'

'You *evacuate* rigs before a hurricane hits,' Farrell put in. 'You don't *stay* on them!'

Abby gave another of her wintry smiles. 'Relax, boys. This is the most modern, up-to-date rig in existence. The only one of its kind. It's been rated for weather conditions much worse than a hurricane. We won't even notice.'

Beck studied the rig again. It looked pretty solid, but he knew that meant nothing when you were talking about something floating around in a hurricane. He also had very little confidence in Lumos and the money they were likely to have spent on the construction. His eyes fixed on a row of bright orange lifepods that hung from the bottom of the rig. They were a much better prospect than the *Sea Cloud*'s lifeboat. They were watertight, plastic shells, completely enclosed. They would be weatherproof and almost unsinkable. If they could get to one of those . . .

The scene disappeared from view as the helicopter turned to face the rig, coming in on its final approach. The engine roared louder as it tilted and slowed. Then it touched down on the metal platform.

The winch man tugged the side door open. Warm air blew in with such force that Beck was almost knocked off his feet. It was so humid and soaked in moisture that it was like breathing underwater. Billowing clouds as black as a funeral shroud hung low over the rig; it looked like you could just reach out and touch them.

The hurricane was very close indeed.

Abby and James jumped out and hurried away.

Beck got down more slowly and looked around. The platform was a strong metal grille supported from below. Through the regular pattern of holes he could see the sea washing against the legs of the rig, fifty metres down.

A man was then suddenly holding his arm in a grip like steel. He and Farrell were led past the pilot, who was having a shouted conversation with the head of the landing crew.

'Get her refuelled. I want to be back on the mainland when the hurricane hits.'

'We can put her in the hangar. You'll be safe.'

'Speak for yourself! I want her filled up and then I'm out of here!'

Beck and Farrell were pulled towards a tall metal door in the superstructure. There was a red light above it. One of their captors swiped a security dongle past a small sensor on the wall and the light beeped to green. Then they were inside.

CHAPTER 37

The door shut behind them with a clang. Their feet rang on the steel floor as they were led along passages, up and down staircases, further and further into the heart of the rig. There were several more electronically locked doors, all opened with swipe cards. Beck remembered, from the paper that Abby had planted on Steven, that people weren't even supposed to talk about the existence of Island Alpha.

Let alone be on it.

This place was pretty darn secret.

The entire rig hummed with working machinery. A deep bass rhythm pulsed through the structure. Beck wondered if it was the sound of the drill.

One final staircase, one more swipe, and then

they were in what must be the control room. It was lined with flatscreens that were ablaze with coloured graphics. About twenty white-coated men and women sat in front of computer monitors and keyboards. One wall was taken up with computer racks and servers. There was a quiet background hubbub of techno-babble that meant nothing to Beck – not until he heard the words 'controlled eruption'.

'Controlled *what*?' he murmured.

James and Abby were already waiting in the room: Abby was in conversation with one of the crew; James had been left sitting on his own, swinging his feet awkwardly. He glanced up as Beck and Farrell were brought in, then quickly looked away again.

Beck noticed that Abby and James had thrown their lifejackets down in a corner in a wet heap. The guards pushed him and Farrell into the same corner to wait. They looked at each other, and then pulled off their own lifejackets to join the pile.

They obviously weren't going to get a chair, so Beck sat cross-legged on the floor. After a moment Farrell joined him. The guard stood watch, staring sternly at them. No one else paid them any further attention. Once again, Beck looked around. What could they do? There was only one way out – the door they had come in by. Say they managed to get past its electronic lock somehow. They could make a break for it. Then they would be alone on the rig with nowhere to run to.

Maybe they could even take one of the lifepods that he had seen from the helicopter. The hurricane would strike and they would be thrown about like pebbles in a tin can, but they would be away from this place.

Farrell nudged him and Beck turned round. He had been so deep in thought that he hadn't noticed James sidling over to them. The other boy was wide-eyed and sweating. Beck regarded him coldly and waited for him to speak.

'They're . . . they're all real busy with this controlled eruption . . . It's just a safety measure, you know, so we aren't sitting on top of a bomb when the storm hits . . .'

'You didn't come to talk to us about controlled eruptions,' Beck said.

James swallowed. 'No. If you were born into this family too . . . if you knew . . .' James's face crumpled as if he was about to burst into tears. Farrell turned away in disgust.

Beck made his own voice firm but kind. They badly needed an ally. And who was he to judge? Could he say he wouldn't have turned out the same, if Abby Blake had been his mother, and Lumos his family's business?

'James, you don't want us to get hurt, do you? You never really wanted to kill us, did you?'

James shook his head urgently. 'No. *No.* It was just . . . Mum said . . . But— Look, if you do get away, could you . . . you know, could you . . . take me?'

'Where would you go?' Beck started.

'James!' Abby's voice cut across the room. 'Get away from them!'

James gave them a final pleading look and quickly returned to his chair.

'Nice try, son,' Farrell muttered.

'He's terrified,' said Beck. 'Of his mum and his granddad.'

Farrell grunted. 'That's what makes him

dangerous. We can't rely on him. His mum twitches her eyebrow and he's back on her side.'

Beck shifted uncomfortably. The metal floor of the control cabin was cold and hard. He reached for the nearest lifejacket in the pile behind them and pulled it over so that he could use it as a cushion. 'But do you think we can get away?'

'I sure don't plan to hang around for Granddad, son. I'm pretty sure he won't have the guts to face us alone. Not without a lot of backup – guys with guns, and bullets that move a whole lot faster than you or me.' The captain glanced over at the control room's single door. One of the crew was just swiping the sensor to let herself out. 'Plus, everything's security controlled, so even if we got out of here somehow, we'd come up short at the next door we reach, and that would be that.'

Beck nodded knowingly.

He was used to surviving in the wild. But surviving in the midst of all this technology seemed to require a whole new set of skills that he just didn't have.

He tried to think logically.

OK, he thought to himself. *Use the same principles of survival . . . just in a different environment. Protection. Rescue. Water. Food. OK, Protection – and this floor is freezing cold. Let's deal with that first, Beck Granger.*

He spread out the lifejacket and arranged it so that the straps and buckles wouldn't stick into him. His thumb brushed against something hard under the plastic surface. Whatever it was, it was in the front pocket. He looked down and thought he saw a familiar outline. Suddenly his heart was pounding, because he was pretty certain he knew what it was.

He slid his fingers in to retrieve it, and they came upon a cold metal loop. Slowly, not drawing any attention to himself, he withdrew Abby's ring. On his advice she had taken it off and put it in the pocket of the lifejacket, so as not to attract sharks. And here it was now.

He gave Farrell a nudge and briefly held the ring out in the palm of his hand, before closing his fingers around it again.

The captain seemed unimpressed. 'Very pretty.'

'Yes, but don't you remember . . . ?' Beck

dropped his voice to a whisper, though it would have been difficult for anyone to overhear them anyway. 'This is how she sabotaged the ship's systems! It's a microcomputer, remember? It could work again. If we crash the rig's systems, maybe the doors will open?'

Farrell suddenly looked very interested. He shot a glance at the banks of computers. They were on the other side of the control room.

'Any place like this will have a failsafe,' he said; 'something goes wrong and everything unlocks so no one gets trapped. You think we could do it here?'

'Maybe,' Beck whispered.

'And then what?'

'Try and make it to a lifepod. Maybe even the helicopter.' Beck honestly didn't know, and he hated not having a plan. But the one thing he did know was that anything was better than sitting around waiting for Granddad Blake to deal with them.

'How did she make it work? On the ship?'

Beck screwed up his face, trying to remember what had happened on the ship's bridge that night. He was sure Abby hadn't done anything.

'She just . . . kind of . . . stood there. James said it's a Bluetooth computer. Maybe it just picks up the nearest computer automatically and does its stuff.'

'Nuh-uh.' Farrell shook his head. 'She'd be wiping out computers left, right and centre just by walking past them. There has to be more to it than that.'

'But she did,' Beck insisted in frustration. 'She just stood there and tapped . . .'

And then he saw it, clear as day. She had tapped – once, twice, three times – and *then* the screens had gone dead.

'It's the tapping. It has to be. Some motion-sensitive detector inside sets it off.'

'Maybe.' Farrell still looked sceptical. 'Sounds like our only chance. But the nearest computers are on the other side of the room.' He nodded over at them. 'They won't let us near them.'

'So we need a diversion.' Beck knew just the thing. Slowly, casually, not attracting anyone's attention – including the guard who now had his back turned to them, watching the technicians – he dug into the pocket of his trousers and pulled out the second of the lifeboat's two flares. Abby had used one of them to attract the helicopter. He had the other.

Farrell's eyes lit up. 'Son, I do like the way you think.' He gave a final look around. 'No time like the present.'

'Nope,' Beck agreed.

He aimed the flare at the roof, took a deep breath, and pulled the tab.

CHAPTER 38

The flare went off with a noise like a shot that echoed off the metal walls.

A mini fireball brighter than the sun, it ricocheted from the roof, bounced down to the floor, skidded across the room, struck a wall, and then bounced back again.

Red smoke started to billow out like a mini power station on steroids.

Crew and technicians jumped and scrambled out of the way with shouts of alarm. The flare burned images into the eyeballs of anyone who looked straight at it. One glimpse was enough to blind any-one for the next thirty seconds.

Which all suited Beck just fine. The moment he pulled the tab, he had leaped towards the computers. He desperately hoped he had guessed right about how to make the ring work. He was going to look mighty stupid if he was wrong, and the Lumos people would not be in a forgiving frame of mind.

He picked what looked like the most important bit of kit and tapped the ring three times against it. *Come on, come on, come on!*

He heard someone shout, 'Hey!' At the same moment, a row of LEDs that had been green turned suddenly red. Other lights that had been pulsing in a slow, regular way suddenly began to flicker randomly.

The light over the door went out and the noise of a blaring klaxon filled the room. Beck ran towards the door, where Farrell was already waiting.

The guard was running towards the flare still hissing violently on the floor, belching out clouds of coloured red smoke.

Everyone else was clustered around one of the computers and shouting incomprehensible techno-speak at each other. He could only understand a few words:

'The regulators have gone down!'

'We have no suppression . . .'

'Loss of control . . .'

Abby was in the midst of the hubbub. James now stood terrified to one side. Beck's eyes met his, and he ventured a nervous, admiring grin.

Farrell tugged at Beck's arm. 'Come on! We *really* need to get out of here.'

'But . . .' Beck protested. He could still hear James's desperate plea: *Could you take me?*

'No buts.' Farrell hauled him out of the control room and almost threw him down the corridor in his haste. Beck stumbled against the metal wall, and snatched his hand away in surprise. The metal was trembling. 'If you remember, those guys back there were in the middle of handling a controlled eruption of the methane hydrate.'

'Fair point,' Beck shouted dryly over the noise and confusion.

A klaxon blared out of a speaker above them and an amplified human voice echoed around the rig: '*All hands brace, all hands brace . . .*'

Farrell had to shout over the announcement.

'And if I understand correctly, they just lost control.'

Beck swallowed. 'The methane hydrate . . . that's erupting . . .'

'. . . is right beneath the rig. Yes. So, come on.'

Beck couldn't stop to think about what he'd done. Now the whole corridor was shaking. He was aware of a low bass rumble at the very edges of his hearing. Rising above it he dimly heard human voices and shouts of alarm. And then the rig rocked as if a giant hand had struck it. The floor lurched and became a slope. Beck and Farrell found themselves staggering downhill. Then they fell flat on their faces as the floor moved up again. A mighty roar filled their ears. Beck had heard a volcano erupting before: this was louder. He was right on top of the sound. It went on and on and on, and the whole rig shook and shuddered with it. Another noise joined the cacophony – an enormous creaking and groaning of tortured metal. It was like the noises from the depths of the sinking *Sea Cloud*, but a hundred times worse.

They passed a sign pointing to the lifepods.

'Uh . . .' Beck hesitated.

Farrell shook his head. 'Everyone will be heading

for them. We'll still be in Lumos's control. We need the helicopter. If it's still here.'

The klaxon still blasted out its regular, rhythmic alarm call. The same voice spoke again: '*All hands brace, here comes another . . .*'

It was even worse than last time. The floor was snatched away beneath them, and then it slammed back up into them even as they were falling. All the breath was knocked out of Beck's lungs. His eyes met Captain Farrell's. Wincing and groaning with pain, they picked themselves up again.

'*All hands abandon rig! All hands abandon rig!*'

CHAPTER 39

They were almost knocked flat again when a tide of panicking men and women tore past them down the corridor, heading for the lifepods.

Good luck to them, Beck thought. He wouldn't want to be in one of those things, pitching and tossing in waves, and then torn apart by a massive underwater explosion.

One more flight of steps, and then they were at a familiar-looking metal door. Farrell shouldered it open and they staggered out onto the helipad.

Beck's heart sang. The helicopter was still there. The pilot was just climbing in. He looked back, saw them, and gestured abruptly: *Hurry up!*

A strong wind whipped against their faces – the precursor of the coming storm. The sea around

Island Alpha foamed and heaved as they hurried across the lurching platform. The rig tilted, and tilted again, and this time showed no sign of stabilizing. The forces below the surface were taking chunks out of its metal legs. The man was already clambering back into the cockpit. The helicopter's powerful turbines fired up – a high-pitched whine that rose and rose as the rotors began to turn. If Beck remembered right, it took about a minute before a helicopter's engines were fully up to speed so that it could lift off. It was going to be a long minute.

His foot was on the step up into the cabin when he stopped and looked back.

Farrell stared at him as if he was mad. 'Beck? What's the problem?'

'James . . .' Beck gasped. 'He asked us to take him with us.'

'James can look after himself— Where are you going?'

Beck took a couple of steps back towards the superstructure. He just couldn't leave like this. Farrell was right about James – he was weak, and afraid. Half of what had happened could have been avoided if the boy had just stood up to his mother and grandfather. But James had asked Beck to take him, and that must have taken every atom of courage he had. He had said what he did because he knew Beck – he had read about his adventures, and now he had survived one with him. James had trusted Beck to do something. Beck just couldn't betray that trust.

The door ahead flew open, and Beck felt a huge grin start to spread across his face, because there was James. A sense of relief gushed through him like a spring of cold water.

But James was stumbling forward, and there, behind him, was Abby. One hand clutched the collar of her son's shirt. Her eyes were wild and her face was contorted with hate. But Beck's attention focused on the gun that was waving about in her other hand.

She saw Beck and her eyes narrowed. She pointed the gun straight at him and fired.

CHAPTER 40

Beck threw himself to one side.

The bullet pinged off the metal deck several metres away. Abby was firing single-handed. The gun's recoil and the shaking rig meant that it was very unlikely she could actually hit anything more than a few metres away.

'No!' James cried out and threw himself at his mother, spoiling her chance of taking another shot. She struck out with the handle of the gun and he dropped to the deck, clutching his face. She took aim again. This time she used both hands, feet apart, aiming like a professional marksman.

Beck was staring straight down the barrel. His heart pounded and he felt time slow down. He couldn't jump faster than a bullet. He would have to leap *just before* she pulled the trigger . . .

Just then, as if by Divine intervention, Island Alpha shook with the worst blow yet. Tortured metal shrieked in protest. A cloud of spray and steam erupted through the grating of the helipad. Beck and Abby both fell to their knees, and Beck heard another shot go wild. Beneath the pad, chunks of the rig were falling away, tumbling down into the heaving water as if in slow motion.

Metal from the rig's drilling tower fell onto the deck, clanging and grinding. Beck's eyes went wide as he caught something moving rapidly down in his peripheral vision. A metal strut had sheared away from the superstructure. He opened his mouth instinctively to shout a warning, but it was too late. Abby cried out, a high-pitched scream of pain, as the strut smashed into her, pinning her to the deck, sending the gun skidding away. Her face was contorted with agony as she lay with the strut across her hips.

'*Mum!*' James cried. He grabbed the free end of the strut and tried to lift it. He turned a pleading face to Beck. 'Help! Please!'

Beck could only wonder at the emotions that must be tearing James apart inside. He was hurting, his soul bent and twisted by his upbringing, just wanting to be free . . . but he was also a son who couldn't bear to see his mother in mortal pain.

And neither could Beck. He hurried forward to lend his strength to James's – though he took the precaution of kicking the dropped gun over the edge of the platform first.

Abby must have been in agony. Beck could see from the way she lay that her pelvis must be broken, the bones probably cracked in at least a couple of places. But apart from that one cry when the strut hit her, she didn't make a sound. Her face was sheet white and drawn, but the fury still blazed in her eyes.

She fixed her hate-filled gaze on Beck. '*You* did this,' she hissed.

It was like she was trying to inject poison into his mind. To drag him down into her world of guilt and suspicion. For half a second it almost worked. Thoughts began to crowd in on Beck. This rig, about to be torn apart by explosions that he had caused because *he* had sabotaged the computers . . .

But he hadn't asked to be here. He had been trying to escape. He was only here because this woman – whose life he was trying to save – hated him and wanted to kill him. And *he* hadn't been stupid enough to drill for a highly unstable and explosive substance in the first place. This was so *not* his fault.

'Get over yourself,' he muttered, and put everything he could into heaving at the strut.

'*Beck!*' Farrell was crouching beside him, shouting over the sound of the explosions and the helicopter engines and the storm. 'The helicopter is set to leave – right now! We have to go!'

'Give me a hand with this!' Beck shouted.

'You'd need five men to lift that. Come on, we need to go!'

'But . . .' *Never say die*, Beck told himself furiously. He cast his eyes around hopelessly.

The helicopter! If they could get a chain, and tie one end to the strut and the other to the helicopter, then maybe the helicopter could lift it off . . .

Farrell grabbed his arm. 'Bring James and come *now*!' He looked coldly down at Abby. 'No offence, lady.'

But then Abby grabbed James violently by the arm. 'If this rig is going down, then we all go down!' she shouted.

'I'm not leaving James – or Abby! We are all getting out of here.' Beck threw his entire strength into pushing against the strut. It wouldn't budge.

He bellowed in frustration as he failed to shift it. '*Aargh!*'

And then, to his horror, he felt Farrell's arms wrap around his chest and lift him bodily away.

'*No!*' he howled. He struggled and kicked as the captain heaved him across the platform, but Farrell was bigger and stronger than him. If he'd found any kind of purchase, he'd have been able to fight back, but Farrell held him up off the ground all the way. The captain threw him into the helicopter cabin and clambered in after him, all in one movement. Beck landed with a thud and immediately scrambled to his feet to leap back out – but then he heard the engines roar, and then the helicopter rapidly lifted away.

Beck fell back into the cabin. Now he was struggling against the helicopter's acceleration, but again he flung himself towards the open door.

Farrell brought him down in a tackle. He landed half in, half out of the helicopter, with Farrell's weight pinning his legs.

'We're done!' the captain shouted. Beck could already see that it was true. They were ten metres up from the platform, and rising. He would break his neck, and that would be no help to anyone.

Farrell helped him slide back into the cabin and Beck picked himself up, glowering back at the captain and pushing away his helping hand. He crouched in the cabin door and looked back in despair at the rig.

Island Alpha was leaning over to one side, the ocean foaming white beneath it. Underwater eruptions threw clouds of steam up and over it, as if the sea was trying to hide the fact that the rig was slowly disintegrating. Cranes, cabins, girders peeled away and tumbled into the water. Then all at once the sea rose up, a massive cloud of boiling, billowing steam, and out of this an orange fireball erupted, engulfing the rig once and for all.

The shock wave struck the helicopter, and the aircraft lurched, spinning wildly as if about to fall out of the sky. Beck was hurled back into the cabin. By the time it had stabilized and he had got back to the door, there was no more Island Alpha, just gradually subsiding foam.

The sky beyond it was completely dark as the hurricane moved ever closer.

CHAPTER 41

'*Our staff are all experts who are fully aware of the dangers involved in their work. They are highly trained and capable of handling a situation like this. The evacuation of Island Alpha was a textbook procedure.*'

The TV screen in Beck's hotel room just showed an empty expanse of ocean. The sea was calm, the waves blue and sparkling.

Then the picture switched to an image of a man in a smart grey suit, standing outside a high-tech office building in downtown Miami. He had a circle of white hair around his otherwise bald head. His face was lean, his eyes narrow and shrewd. The caption read: EDWIN BLAKE.

Beck hated him on sight.

Blake was surrounded by a gaggle of reporters, but one in particular had his microphone in the man's face.

'*But there was one casualty,*' the reporter said.

Blake paused, then nodded. '*I have spoken to some of the survivors. They have all agreed that my daughter Abby sacrificed her life through her insistence on helping others first.*' He paused and drew in a breath that shuddered slightly.

It was a flawless fake performance of a man struggling with grief. Coming from anyone else, it would have taken Beck in completely. Knowing what he did about the founder of Lumos, he didn't believe a word of it.

'*She was the most senior Lumos executive on board Island Alpha and her first thought was for everyone who worked for the company. It's typical of the way she performed her job. She will be deeply missed . . .*'

'*Can you dismiss the possibility of sabotage?*'

'*By no means. We are considering all possibilities.*' Blake's hawk-like eyes bored into the camera, and into Beck. Blake was addressing anyone watching the broadcast, but there was no doubt in Beck's mind that he was speaking to just one person. '*Obviously we will be co-operating fully with the American authorities in their investigation. But let me emphasize, if sabotage is proved to have occurred – if, for example, it turns out that someone hacked the computers that monitored the pressures inside the pipeline during a controlled eruption – then no stone will be left unturned in seeking out the perpetrator. No stone at all. There is nowhere to hide. It's only a very small planet. We will find you and bring you to justice.*'

'Yes, we will have justice,' Beck murmured. He walked out onto the balcony while Blake continued with his performance.

'*I would like to emphasize that there was no environmental damage – Lumos takes its responsibilities towards our planet very seriously – and I can only repeat that this was a textbook procedure . . .*'

'Turn it off!' Beck said quietly. He leaned on the balcony rail and looked out over Miami beach, and the sea beyond it.

A moment later, his Uncle Al came to join him at the balcony.

After the *Sea Cloud* was reported missing, Al had been on the first available flight to Florida. He and Beck must have set foot on American soil at almost the same time.

'So, did James make it?' Uncle Al said.

Beck grunted. 'Maybe. I pray so.'

And he did. He would remember, for the rest of his life, the look of shock and betrayal on James's face as Farrell had dragged Beck away.

If James was found alive, Beck would rejoice. If he turned up dead, or was never found at all, Beck would be distraught. He would feel he had betrayed him. He would be grieving not only for the boy who had died, but for the boy who had never lived – the decent, likeable, honest guy that James could have been.

He couldn't grieve for Abby. He was sad about her death, because no one deserved to die like that. But he couldn't grieve.

The helicopter pilot had given his version of events to the authorities when he landed at Miami.

No one disputed it, not even Beck. The man was just hired to fly the machine; he had been about to depart for the mainland; he had picked up Farrell and Beck before Island Alpha collapsed and brought them with him.

Beck and Farrell had given the approximate location of the uninhabited island they had found to the US Coastguard. They were looking for it now, hoping to retrieve Steven's body – if it was still there after the hurricane had passed through.

'The taxi's here,' Al said.

Beck took one last look at the tropical scene in front of him. Bright sun. Palm trees. Sun, sea and sand. Men, women and children sunbathing or splashing in the waves. 'Let's get out of here,' he said.

There was one more ordeal to face, and it started the moment the lift doors opened onto the lobby. Flash bulbs exploded in front of Beck's face.

'Beck! Beck! Did you hear what Lumos had to say?'

'Do you have anything to add?'

'What were your feelings when you saw the rig collapse . . . ?'

Al pushed his way through the scrum of reporters. He used their suitcases as a battering ram and wasn't too bothered about who he hit. Beck followed in the path that his uncle cleared. Both of them just muttered a curt 'No comment.'

They had thought of commenting, plenty. Beck had a lot to say. But who would believe it? He was one boy.

He had talked to Farrell. The captain had already had a polite call from a Lumos lawyer. Smiling, not threatening at all, not saying anything that could be held against him, the lawyer had pointed out some hard truths. Farrell was a disgraced ship's captain, already suspected of losing one ship through negligence, now with a second lost ship on his record. Lumos could – if it wanted – wreck his career for ever. Their lawyers and PR people could make sure that he would never, ever work again. He wouldn't stand a chance against the kind of attack that their resources could buy.

Farrell was no coward. He was prepared to throw

everything away, if he could join up with Beck and fight back.

Beck had told the captain that he had done his bit to hurt Lumos. This was no longer his fight.

But Beck wasn't afraid of Lumos. They couldn't hurt him like they could hurt Farrell. Lumos couldn't hurt his career prospects. He intended to work for Green Force when he left school, and Lumos would have to deal with it.

As James had put it, back on the island: he was also going to join the 'family firm'.

Their cases were stowed in the boot of the taxi. Beck and Al climbed into the back and pulled the doors shut.

'Airport, please,' Al said. The taxi pulled away from the mob behind it.

Neither of them spoke for a while. Then Al broke the silence.

'We'll be just in time for Christmas,' he said. 'I warn you I haven't had much time for shopping. You're looking at an empty stocking.'

Beck managed to give a tired smile. 'Surprise me,' he said, and settled back in his seat.

He was looking forward to Christmas. He would enjoy the normality of December in England. Let it be cold, let it be wet. He needed the break – he needed time to relax, and recharge, and regain his strength for the battle that was to come.

Blake's last words still rang in his ears. Blake must already know that Beck was still alive. Lumos would come for him again.

But not if Beck came for them first.

EPILOGUE

The blunt tip of the stick skidded off the base plate again. The bedraggled, bruised boy screamed and flung it as far away as he could. There was no one but gulls to see or hear him.

'How does he do it? How does he do it?'

Beck had made it look so simple. Dig the fire drill into the base plate. Spin it. Fire happened.

Every time James tried it, the drill just took on a life of its own.

But he was going to make it work. He forced himself to get to his feet and walk along the debris-strewn beach until he had found the stick again. Then he went back to the pile that would become a fire. Sobbing with frustration, and the pain of his cracked, blistered palms, he started again.

It might have been the same island they had landed on with the lifeboat. He honestly had no idea. Any recognizable features had been obliterated by the storm.

The helicopter had been whirring, screaming. Beck had been dragged away, and left James to die.

Beck had betrayed him. He had lied. He had let himself be saved and left him to die.

James, weeping, had been throwing all his strength at the strut that pinned his mother down. And then he had seen the man – another member of Island Alpha's crew, making one final check of the rig before heading for the lifepods. He had done to James what Farrell had done to Beck – picked him up and carried him off. Except that James had been screaming for his mother all the way.

The man had thrown him into a lifepod and had been about to climb in when the rig blew. James was pretty sure he had been knocked out by the blast. He had a vague memory of noise, and pain. At the heart of the explosion, he must have rattled around inside the pod like a pea in a shell. But it was a very different piece of technology to the lifeboat that had carried them away from the *Sea Cloud*. Its tough plastic shell had sealed up automatically when it detached from Island Alpha and the explosion hadn't cracked it.

James hadn't died.

Although part of him had. The part that could feel joy, and laughter, and love – had died on Island Alpha.

And when he woke up, he'd found the lifepod beached on the island. It was still there, further down the beach. Bright orange, so no one could miss it. Packed full of survival rations, so James wouldn't starve. He knew someone would come for him eventually.

But James wasn't going to rely on anyone else from now on. He would survive on his own skills. Hence the fire. He had to do it. He had to learn how. He had to be strong and tough to follow what he now knew was the path of his life, fuelled by the core of hatred that burned inside him like a nuclear reactor.

He would survive. He would have his revenge. Somehow.

NAVIGATING BY THE STARS

Navigating by the stars – astronavigation – is one of the oldest navigation methods known to man. It can certainly be a very in-depth study, but a small amount of knowledge can be a big help if you're navigating at night because you can use the stars to determine direction. Which stars you use depends on which hemisphere you're in.

The northern hemisphere

In the northern hemisphere, the most useful star is the North Star (Polaris). If you walk towards this star, you will always be heading north; and from that you can work out the other directions.

Contrary to popular myth, the North Star isn't the brightest star in the sky. It is, however, easy to locate if you learn to recognize three constellations: Ursa Minor (the Little Dipper), Ursa Major (the Big Dipper or the Plough) and Cassiopeia.

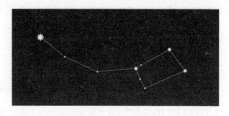

The North Star is the final star in the handle of the saucepan shape of Ursa Minor (right).

However, it is not always possible to see Ursa Minor.

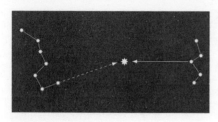

If this is the case, you need to look for Ursa Major and Cassiopeia (left).

If you draw a straight line from the two stars at the end of Ursa Major's 'bowl', you will come to Polaris. It is about four times the length between the last two stars of Ursa Major along the same line of direction. Cassiopeia looks like a wonky W or M on its side. If you follow a line straight out from the centre star of Cassiopeia, you'll reach Polaris. It's about halfway between the two constellations.

The southern hemisphere

Polaris can't be seen from most of the southern hemisphere, so there you need to use a different constellation, the Southern Cross. This will help you work out which way is south.

Imagine extending the long axis of the Southern Cross to five times its length. From this imaginary point in the sky, follow a vertical line down towards the earth. The direction from where you are to that point on the ground will be south.

BEAR GRYLLS is one of the world's most famous adventurers. After spending three years in the SAS he set off to explore the globe in search of even bigger challenges. He has climbed Mount Everest, crossed the Sahara Desert and circumnavigated Britain on a jet-ski. His TV shows have been seen by more than 1.2 billion viewers in more than 150 countries. In 2009, Bear became Chief Scout to the Scouting Association. He lives in London and Wales with his wife Shara and their three sons: Jesse, Marmaduke and Huckleberry.

MISSION SURVIVAL

GOLD OF THE GODS

Would you survive?

Beck Granger is lost in the jungle with no food,
no compass, and no hope of rescue.

But Beck is no ordinary teenager – he's
the world's youngest survival expert.
If anyone can make it out alive, he can.

MISSION SURVIVAL

WAY OF THE WOLF

Would you survive?

A fatal plane crash. A frozen wilderness.
The world's youngest survival expert
is in trouble again . . .

MISSION SURVIVAL

SANDS OF THE SCORPION

Would you survive?

Beck Granger is about to face his toughest survival
challenge yet – the Sahara Desert. Blistering sun
and no water for hundreds of miles . . .

Can he survive the heat and make it out alive?

MISSION⊕SURVIVAL

TRACKS
OF THE TIGER

Would you survive?

A volcano eruption leaves Beck stranded
and alone in the jungle. Beck must use
all his skills to survive the dangers of
the jungle – can he get to safety?

MUD, SWEAT AND TEARS

This is the thrilling story of everyone's favourite
real-life action man – Bear Grylls.

Find out what it's like to take on mountaineering,
martial arts, parachuting, life in the SAS – and all
that nature can throw at you!

MISSION SURVIVAL

TRACKS
OF THE TIGER

Would you survive?

A volcano eruption leaves Beck stranded
and alone in the jungle. Beck must use
all his skills to survive the dangers of
the jungle – can he get to safety?

MUD, SWEAT AND TEARS

This is the thrilling story of everyone's favourite
real-life action man – Bear Grylls.

Find out what it's like to take on mountaineering,
martial arts, parachuting, life in the SAS – and all
that nature can throw at you!